Borderline Freaks MC #1

MariaLisa deMora

Edited by Hot Tree Editing

Proofreading by Whiskey Jack Editing

First Published 2019

ISBN 13: 978-1-946738-46-2

DEDICATION

Our debt to the heroic men and valiant women in the service of our country can never be repaid. They have earned our undying gratitude. America will never forget their sacrifices. ~ President Harry S. Truman

To the service men and women who've given so much, including the ultimate sacrifice, and the ones they've left behind: Thank you.

CONTENTS

ACKNOWLEDGMENTS

This story is the culmination of my brain working overtime while riding on multiple memorial rides for fallen warriors. In watching the emotional responses and facial expressions of the riders and passengers who roll alongside me, I've been blessed to witness an etched grief that will not pass. When we ride for a warrior, no matter when or how they died, we live for them.

It doesn't matter if the one we're honoring was personally known by the individuals riding, because in those moments the dead belong to us in a way people may never understand. It grieves me deeply that we've buried far too many of our brightest and best men and women, and while their service is necessary and fills me with gratitude, I wish there were another way.

This story is also in response to too many Memorial Days and Veterans Days where the media is quick to parade images of grieving spouses, timed to gain the most viewers. Obscenely invading the private moments spent remembering what their life once was, flaying them open for the world to see.

Amanda and Alex have a hell of a story to tell, if you care to listen. While this book is first in the Borderline Freaks MC series, it sits in a unique space because it's also an isolated tale of loss. There was so much grief my shoulders bowed carrying it to the page, but it's also about a deep and abiding love. So much love, that full and flowing emotion must be experienced to be believed.

To those who have served or are serving, and to their families—I offer you my gratitude and thanks. Thank you for a job well done, for taking up the watch in my place. For keeping the security of our country under duress and in the face of adversary. For those who stay behind, thank you for supporting your loved ones as they willingly place themselves in harm's way.

Your sacrifices are seen and appreciated.

Woofully yours,
~ML

Service and Sacrifice

"Thank you for your service" is what we're taught to say to military men and women in gratitude for our freedoms won at their expense. Less often do we thank their families, those left behind to hold down the fort, to manage the day-to-day struggle of keeping everything up in the air until their loved one returns.

When you can't count on anyone else to save you, there's only one real choice.

Amanda lost her husband to war. Alex lost part of himself. Through a series of glancing encounters, Amanda and Alex find reasons to continue on. And together, they'll discover hope and peace can be found in the most unexpected of places.

One

Amanda

Amanda leaned against the side of the car she'd borrowed from a neighbor and watched carefully as the numbers ticked up in the pump display. Her palm was slick against the ratcheted handle as she slowed the dispensing rate, then slowed it again, waiting until the total hit the even twenty bucks she had in her wallet. She'd retrieved the money and just returned the nozzle to the holder before turning to twist the gas cap into place when she heard the hum. Or felt it, really.

A throbbing thrum of something tickled the soles of her feet; then the racket grew louder, sending tiny thrills of shivery sensation up her legs and into her belly. It seemed to echo off every building around, the sound folding back in and on itself until there was nothing except this primal thunder. The first bikes appeared moments later, and she steadied herself against the car door as she watched the double line of vehicles slow, signal, and swoop into the station. They split into a pattern only they recognized, machines and men pulling up three and four deep on every pump.

She looked left and saw a pair of bikes had appeared just in front of the car, unsmiling men staring at her. Not a glare, nothing overtly threatening, but more as if she didn't matter. As if her existence factored so little they scarcely noticed her except for the fact she stood beside the only pump blocked by a car. She glanced right and found two more bikes a short distance off, barely giving her enough room to back up and leave. She nodded her thanks, getting one chin lift in response before she clambered into the car.

Then right back out, because she still had the money clutched in her hand. She stared at the two men in front of the car, but they were no longer looking at her, heads turned to talk to each other, pointedly ignoring her polite wave. She looked the other direction and held up her hand, pointed at the money, then at the door of the station. Chin lift guy shook his head and made a shooing motion with one hand while the man next to him laughed, lips splitting in soundless humor at her predicament.

"Park, then pay."

Amanda shrieked and whirled, one hand coming up to cover her throat in a useless defensive move. One of the other men had dismounted from his bike and was standing right in front of her. A black bandana was wrapped around his head, and dark sunglasses kept his eyes from view as he leaned in aggressively and repeated himself. "Park." He shoved his hand towards the store, pointer finger extended. "Then pay."

He smelled of oil and gasoline, and faintly of an attractive something she couldn't define. Wide shoulders and massive arms strained the seams of the jacket he wore, folds creased into the elbows telling of long hours of wear. With a short, untrimmed beard and a tattoo crawling up the side of his neck, he looked every bit the kind of terrifying man she'd avoided all her life.

Amanda Stewart didn't go for bad boys. She'd never once walked on the wild side. Married at eighteen to her high school sweetheart, she lived a safe and sane, and predictable life. Her family had moved on, parents retiring to warmer states and her brothers scattering to the winds, but she still lived in the same town where they'd all grown up. In fact, other than a rare trip, she'd never ventured outside the state where she'd been born and was so okay with that even her siblings laughed at her.

She might have carefully crafted her life as best she could, but everything else was in disarray. Almost five years ago her husband had come home unexpectedly, his travel unscheduled, all their future plans waylaid by an enemy sniper in the mountains of Afghanistan. Amanda had sat stiffly on the first pew of the same church where they'd married, and then again in a folding chair next to the raw earth mounded beside a freshly dug hole, accepting the condolences of their friends and family, his commander, and a few of the men who'd walked so many miles alongside him. The sun was past zenith when the startling booms of the salute rang out and had dropped to kiss the horizon before she'd given in to the urging of her brothers and swayed to her feet to toss in her handful of clay. Folded flag in her lap, she hadn't been refusing to leave so much as she just couldn't imagine going anywhere else.

A year later, their house had gone back to the bank, because without the active duty pay, she couldn't afford it. She'd held on to the car, scrimping and scraping money together every month for the too-large payment, while she'd bounced among her dwindling friends from couch to guest room—and for a short time before she'd gotten a small efficiency apartment, to the back seat of the car. Not that anyone knew about that last bit, because she'd been determined to not let anyone pity her.

But now even the car was in danger, because the transmission had threatened to give out last week. The shop owner was an old classmate, and he'd promised to hold the car for another month to give her time to pay for the repairs, even after he'd told her the vehicle wasn't worth the cost.

It didn't matter to her, because Martin had picked it out, had loved it, had wanted it. And what Martin wanted, he got, in so many things. Beautiful, faithful wife, check.

Ostentatious house, absolutely. Impractical car, you got it. Military career always volunteering for dangerous missions, outstanding choice, sir, there you go.

So here she was at nearly thirty, borrowing a car to drive to her low-wage job at the big-box store one town over. Still pinching pennies because putting more gas in the car meant fewer groceries in her already skimpy pantry. In so many ways she felt like life had passed her by, misplaced in the wake of young love and stability, of service and loss.

And the man standing too close, who looked angry now, was terrifying. "Jesus, lady, you deaf or something? We need that pump." He reached up and took off the sunglasses, tucking one temple piece into the neck of his shirt, exposed now because he'd unzipped his jacket at some point. *Probably when he teleported over here.* His green eyes were flat and cold, filled with a heavy dose of the don't-give-a-shit attitude she was sure he had been born with.

Wordlessly, Amanda held out the money, not certain what she hoped to accomplish with this mute appeal. Maybe to have him back off, or understand, or see how frightened she was, fingers shaking so the bill looked nearly ready to take flight.

"Yeah, I get that you gotta pay, lady. Just—" He gestured behind him again, towards the front of the shop. "Park first."

She looked to the side. There were bikes everywhere, scattered in groups and wavering lines across the parking lot, and she didn't see a way to drive past them to the slotted spaces in front of the store. Glancing behind, she saw the other two bikes had rolled closer, and she felt a wave of panic when she realized she was effectively blocked in. She whirled and shoved the money at him again, fist clenched to hold the trembling at bay.

He stared at her a moment, crinkles in the corners of his eyes becoming more pronounced, gaze never leaving her face. Then he turned his head to shout over his shoulder, "FNG." Curls of hair escaped from the back of the bandana, dark blond and thick.

That acronym, that title, was familiar. Martin and his friends had joked about the scrubs in their platoon, the newbies, fresh off the farm sometimes: Fucking New Guy. Amanda studied the patches on the man's jacket and saw another thing that felt familiar. A military insignia that matched the memorized one worn by Martin in his dress uniform. "Oorah," she whispered, and he whipped his head back to her. "Thank you for your service, Marine."

This time, instead of lady, she earned, "Ma'am. My duty and honor." Something Martin had said in response to people at diners or grocery stores—she looked around—or gas stations, when they'd interrupt whatever he and she had been doing to offer their thanks.

Duty and honor. She scrubbed at her nose with the back of her wrist, then absently looked down and ran a thumb over the tattoo on the underside of that wrist. Right over where her pulse was strongest, where the skin was weak and the blood ran hot. Where the blade had missed the intended target, her eyes blinded by overflowing tears.

The man reached out and cradled her hand in his, and she looked up to see the top of his head fringed by more of those curls. Chin angled down, he was studying her tattoo, and any question of whether he knew the meaning was gone when he lifted his face to hers. Eyes narrowed, he stared hard at her a minute, and she realized at some point he'd started examining her tattoo by touch, moving along her skin so the pad of his thumb now traced the scar.

"Brother?" The lifting sound at the end told her he was guessing the who but knew the what and why, and she took a breath because it had been a long time since someone had just known like that. Since there'd been a nearly wordless understanding.

"Husband." She swallowed around the words that wanted to escape after, forcing them down before they got free. *Lover. Best friend. Soul mate.*

"I'm sorry for your loss." He gave her wrist a squeeze, then retained his hold, keeping her in place. He folded her fingers around the bill and told her, "Don't worry about the gas. It'll be on me, ma'am. Where was he?"

"Helmand." If this man had served overseas, he would know that name—and from the grimace on his face, she knew she was right. "Thank you."

"How long?" A man stepped up behind him, and over his shoulder the Marine gave a brusque order. "Put her gas on the card, man, my tab." Then his intense eyes were back on her and she stared at him as he repeated his question. "How long?"

Amanda closed her eyes. "One thousand, eight hundred, and twenty-six days."

"Oh, honey." Strong arms wrapped around her, and it was so good, so unbelievably good that Amanda let herself sink into the embrace, uncaring how rough the zipper felt against her cheek, how irresponsible it might be to allow a stranger to cradle her like this, because someone was granting her permission to give up being strong for one minute. "This week, huh?"

She nodded. "Tomorrow."

It took a minute, and when it came, the words were gritted out, voice trembling with something like anger. "Suckass kind of anniversary."

She nodded again.

Another period of silence filled only with her heartbeat, his friends' murmured conversations and bursts of laughter seeming far away. "What'll you do to remember him?"

"Visit the cemetery." Something she did every week without fail. Rain, snow, heat—it didn't matter. She kept her self-appointed trek where the only certainty was in the solo arrival and lonely vigil.

"The one here in town?" His voice rumbled under her ear, and she felt pressure against the top of her head. "On the highway east of town?"

"Yes. That's where he is." Something his parents hadn't wanted, but she was glad she'd stuck to her decision and that finally her requests had been honored. They would have preferred somewhere bigger, a location they felt more deserving of their son's loss, someplace they could hold up as a proper memorial. But if he'd been across the country, or even in the military cemetery downstate, it would have made her visits more difficult. She pulled in a breath and caught the elusive scent again. This close, it was filled with notes of masculinity she hadn't noticed before. "Thank you." Amanda stepped back and let her arms drop, not even having realized when she'd wrapped them around his waist. *Holding on like he's a life raft*.

He released her, then reached out and trailed fire along her wrist, mapping the scar until he pressed against the semicolon she carried there. "Thank you for your sacrifice."

She ducked her head and settled into the driver seat of the car, surprised when the bikes were gone from in front of her. There were four parked in front of the store, the rest having disappeared sometime during that interlude. The car door closed gently, then two taps on the roof to send her on her way, just like Martin had always done.

Amanda glanced at her mirror as she drove away, seeing the tall man still standing next to the gas pump like a surprising sentinel.

Two

Monk

Alex Waterman watched the old car bounce over the low curb that separated the gas station from the street and traced the woman's route with his gaze until she rolled out of sight. He couldn't remember ever seeing someone carry as much pain and grief while still keeping themselves upright. The look on her face as she'd counted off the days told him how she'd measured the painful hours of each one, holding out hope the next sunrise would prove nightmares didn't exist, rising from her lonely bed to wrestle them to heel. Day after day, and at some point she'd given up on that route, seeking a final solace. Even that had been denied, or she wouldn't have had that damn tattoo to prove how she'd survived.

"Monk, you ready to roll, brother?" Alex looked up and smiled at his club name, brain changing gears until he was fully back in the moment with his patch brothers in the Borderline Freaks Motorcycle Club. He knew Blade, the one who'd spoken, would also be the one who'd moved Monk's bike without having to be asked. "We sent the main column on, just us hung back with you." Unspoken were the questions about the woman, *who* and *why* probably first on their tongues. The problem was Monk wasn't sure what had happened, not really.

One moment he'd been annoyed that a good ride on a good day was being disrupted by a bitch who couldn't be bothered to show the least bit of decency and move her goddamned junker out of the way so they could fuel, and the next he'd been holding her while she breathed through her grief, every swell and collapse of her ribcage pained and rough, like something was killing her slowly from inside.

"Yeah, man. I'm ready."

The rest of the ride, rolling hard and fast to catch up with the group, then through two more fuel stops, and finally halting at a diner everyone liked near the state line, Monk couldn't drag his mind away from the woman. "Husband," she'd said, and infused that single seven-letter word with so much loss it stole away his breath. The expression she'd worn was like and yet unlike every war widow he'd had to see. Personal notifications if he was stateside, and those were the hardest. It didn't matter if they'd looked outside to see who was at the curb; taken unawares, each face carried pain and disbelief and fear. *Jesus*. So much fucking fear. Door flung wide on a scream of "No," or opened gently with children in arms and already tear-streaked faces, women took the news as best they could bear it. Men did too, because he'd had to make more than one distaff notification, too, that their beloved wife, cherished mother, or favored daughter wouldn't be coming home again.

The emotions he'd seen in the woman's face today were grief and acceptance, well past the denial stage. What he'd offered her in the form of a physical connection wasn't his gig. Condolences weren't what he did, unless it was one of *his* men. There'd been too many of those, and he was hella glad those days were in his rearview.

"Monk." At his name, he looked up from the menu at Neptune, another fellow Marine and patch brother. "Woman needs your order, man." Monk blinked, looked around, and realized the place had filled up with his brothers.

"Just the coffee." He knew even that would sour in his stomach, but the idea of eating wasn't appealing. Not right now. Monk offered her the plastic-coated menu, and she pointed to the napkin holder on the table, where he saw three more just like it tucked alongside. Where he'd undoubtedly retrieved the thing from originally. *Fuck*. He tried to smile, nodding as she shifted to the next table. "Thanks."

"Pretty thang" came from beside him, and he glared at Wolf, another double brother he'd served with overseas. His glare apparently wasn't enough of a deterrent, because the man continued in that vein, exactly as Monk would expect. "Gonna go back and tap that pretty thang? Be a Monk no more, brother, about damn time."

Alex had earned the name Monk one night at an epic party where there'd been girls and booze aplenty, nerve-soothing pot in ample quantities, and brotherhood of the highest order. Someone had asked him why he wasn't in line for a woman, and he'd told them all about what it meant to have his PTSD. He rolled his eyes at the memory of that version of Monk, still just known as Waterboy, and he wasn't sure which was worse.

"You wanna know why? You sure? Because I'm fucked in the head." He pulled a face, tongue wagging, finger cocked at his own temple. "Fucked in the head, but can't fuck with the body." Jeans unzipped, he dug his soft cock out and shook it. "ED ain't no joke, man. Little buddy here ain't interested in anything anymore." Gyrating his hips, he helicoptered his dick, the men around him falling out of their chairs laughing. "Uncle Sam won't allow but six little blue pills a month." He pulled up ramrod straight and saluted. "Yes, sir. Thank you, sir. I'll be happy to get a half a dozen hard-ons every thirty, sir." Shoving his member back in his jeans, he finished, "Half the time it's too much work to dick around with." Laughing, he pounded Blade's shoulder. "Get it, dick around with?" Collapsing back into his chair, he said, "So that's why I'm here and not there."

He pointed across the room to where two men were double-teaming a woman, had her squeezed between them as they fucked her ass and pussy hard. "Might as well join a...what's it called for men? A monkery? I don't know. I'm just fucked in the head, man, and these days, not fucked in the flesh."

"No. She's a widow, brother." All three men seated with him froze in place. They knew the significance that word carried and were probably rewriting today's encounter in their own minds with just that single sentence.

Blade pulled in a breath. "She's from there." It was a statement, not a question, but Monk responded as if he'd asked it, nodding slowly. Blade hummed softly, face twisting in remembered grief. "I did an honor ride a few years ago from the base."

The three of them had all been stationed at the local base, Monk the only one who'd settled here to get away from all the baggage he'd wanted to leave behind. A wife, and her not liking being alone ten or eleven months of the year, if they were lucky. Friends, who didn't get why he wasn't the same free spirit they'd known in high school. Family, who looked at him sadly as they patched holes in their walls or paid bail bondsmen cash to retrieve his ass from the most recent round of ridiculous behavior. Bosses as they shook their heads, holding out an envelope to indicate a termination of employment. Establishing a new life here had been a chance at a fresh start, and finding the brotherhood he'd needed in the Borderline Freaks had proved the move to be fate.

Neptune added, "Dude was corps," and Wolf nodded. "Had nearly twenty-two hundred bikes on that ride. Streets and roads were lined for miles and miles with people paying their respects. Flags everywhere. Patriots had point," meaning the local chapter of that national MC had been positioned directly behind the hearse and cars with family, "and we were next in line. Oorah."

"Oorah." The time-worn response to a call to faith and fidelity echoed around the table, Monk's voice the final one to chime in.

"How do you know her?" Blade pushed back in the seat, and Monk looked up to see the waitress coming their way with a tray of drinks.

"Don't. She was having a hard time today, and something clicked, so I knew she was a widow." He met the waitress's eyes and nodded his thanks for the mug of coffee. "Tomorrow's five for her without him."

"Oh, man. Death days are the worst." Neptune reached for the sugar and poured an unhealthy stream into his black coffee. "No wonder she was having a hard time."

"Yeah." Monk glanced around the room, then looked outside at the bright blue sky dotted with white clouds. *No worries there*. He blinked and thought he saw mountains in the distance, but a second blink wiped them away. "No wonder."

Three

Amanda

Amanda twisted in the seat of the parked car and gathered up the things she needed for her vigil. She'd done this often enough to know exactly what made her the right level of comfortable to stay as long as she needed. Blanket to sit on, but not too thick, because Martin's body was surrounded by cold dirt and it was right that she feel some of that. A bottle of water, because the first two years she'd wept so much in the summer sun she'd dehydrated and passed out, waking up hours later with an uneven sunburn on her face that had been hard to explain away. Their wedding book, which had turned into a scrapbook of their lives together. Ritual and known, this was what she did.

She climbed out and sighed as she leaned her weight against the door, bumping it hard enough with her hip to make the latch catch. Then she began the long walk back through the headstones to where Martin's grave was. This too was part of the ritual, because she could have parked within ten feet of the granite that bore his name, but the trek helped Amanda center herself so she didn't lose it as soon as she stood in front of him. Living, breathing—alive, while he was dead.

As she got closer, she noticed a motorcycle parked just down the row from her destination. Big and black, it had angular handlebars and some kind of fabric wrapped around the pipes, nothing shiny about this bike, and it felt even more imposing for that detail. Another twenty feet and she saw something else unusual, a man kneeling next to Martin's grave, one hand placing something in the back pocket of his jeans, the other holding a small flag. As she watched, he reached out and stuck the flag into the ground next to the headstone, adjusting until it stood upright.

This wasn't someone she knew, no one from Martin's family or hers, no friend from school. *He must have served with Martin.* She pulled in a shocked breath, blinking back sudden tears. *No, no, not yet.* Her throat clicked when she swallowed, even as her mouth flooded with bitter saliva because she hadn't prepared for this. Wasn't ready to talk about Martin, to share memories with someone she didn't know, to listen to their stories and their grief. Then he looked up, and with a swirl of relief, she saw it was the man from the gas station. *Stupid.* Of course it would have to be him; she'd talked to him only yesterday and told him what today meant. *I should have recognized the bike.*

"Ma'am." Stilted and formal, he dipped his head toward the gravestone. "Wasn't hard to find. Thought I'd pay my respects." He moved away, stepping into the middle of the little road. "I'll be out of your hair."

"Did you know him? Martin? My husband? Did you know him?" She was overwhelmed with a need to know. Counter to what she'd felt a moment ago when it was a stranger who might have served, she didn't feel this man a stranger any longer. "Martin Stewart?"

"No, ma'am. We weren't posted together that I know of. But he was USMC." He lifted one shoulder and took a step towards his bike. "Corps."

"Makes you family." She nodded. "You don't have to, you know." He paused and looked at her. "Leave, I mean. I don't mind."

"Figured you'd rather time alone." He glanced at the headstone, then back at her. "Mrs. Stewart."

She dipped her chin and broke free from his gaze. It had been so long since anyone called her that, it felt wrong, almost like she was an imposter. "I'm alone all the time. It'd be nice—" She gestured towards the grave. "—for it to not be just me for once."

"Are you sure, ma'am?"

Eyes angled down, she nodded slowly. "I am." She bent to set the water and scrapbook down, then began unfolding the blanket. A shadow fell on her, and she looked up to find him close, reaching out for a corner of the fabric. Together they arranged it as she always did, directly to the side of the place where dirt had once mounded. Once they were seated, she lifted the bottle and apologized. "I only have the one."

"Don't you worry about me. I'm fine." He leaned forwards and plucked a blade of grass, arm propped on one bent knee. "You come out every year?"

"Every week, actually, but I always make sure to come on the anniversary." She spun the lid off and lifted the bottle for a drink. "His parents come on Saturdays or Sundays, when they come, so I always aim at Wednesday."

"You don't get along?" His questions were innocent, skimming along the surface of polite, not knowing the landmines waiting underneath.

"Understatement." She smiled and stretched out a hand, dusting the surface of the stone's base. "They didn't like that we got married so young, and thought I influenced him to join up." Turning her neck, she looked at him. "Opposite from reality, and they probably know it under everything. But it's easier to have someone to be mad at, you know? I can take it. They lost a son, so it's the least I can do." She rested her cheek on her knees. "They wanted him in Arlington, or in the state military cemetery. Someplace more befitting a man of his"—with one hand she made air quotes—"stature." He stared at her steadily, not looking away, taking in everything she had to say. Being the subject of that kind of singular focus from this man felt surprisingly good, comfortable. "And by stature I mean money, their money. Family money. I wanted him here." She turned her head away, staring at the granite etched with his name. "Where I could come see him."

They sat in silence for several minutes, Amanda's memories awash with images of Martin at graduation: from high school, from boot camp, from officer's training. She didn't know what the man spent those minutes thinking or considering, but for her, it was all Martin.

"My name's Amanda," she said, suddenly aware she hadn't introduced herself to this stranger, no matter they were sharing a private moment. "So you can ix-nay on the am-may bit."

He laughed softly, chuckling long past when she thought it should have been funny, so she turned to look at him. A gentle smile quirked his lips sideways. "Ix-nay? Really?"

"Yeah." She sat up straight, staring at him. *He's teasing me*. She gave it right back to him, lifting her chin as she repeated, "Ix-nay."

"Alex Waterman."

"Good to meet you, Alex Waterman."

"Same to you, Amanda Stewart."

An hour passed by before either spoke again. It was Alex who broke the silence, asking a question she'd never fielded before. "How was it for you, being home, before this happened?"

"You mean staying here while he deployed?" She turned to look at him in time to see a tiny nod. "It was okay. I had the house to take care of, and I worked. I missed him, of course, but he missed me, too."

"Did you know he was going to join before you married? Or was that a decision he came to afterwards?"

"Oh, no. I knew from the time we were sophomores he would be in the military. It was what he'd planned and worked towards. He did delayed entry our senior year, and we'd planned on waiting until he'd gotten out of basic to get married. None of this made it through to any conversations with our parents, of course." She laughed.

"Of course." He smiled at her, a full spreading of his lips that changed his face entirely, making him more approachable, softening the hard lines he wore most of the time, and turning up his good-looking level by several notches. She wasn't immune to the fact he was handsome, in that bad boy way that hadn't ever been her go-to for desirability. But this, what they were doing by sitting here to honor Martin, turned any idea that the meeting might be seen as tawdry into a lie, showing instead that it was a brilliant sign of respect for her dead husband. That smile on his face, however, turned the corner from attractive to smoldering hot in a moment. She stared at him until he frowned, losing the grin to an expression of puzzlement. "What?"

"Nothing." She turned away, back to the headstone, feeling as if she'd somehow betrayed Martin by noticing the attractiveness. Which was stupid, because he wasn't around to betray. He was gone, long gone, and the permanence of his not being here struck her hard, like it always did out of the blue. It took her breath away, and in a moment she was crying hard, shoulders shaking as she wrapped her arms around her knees, tucking them close to her chest to try and stop the pain flooding through her.

As he had at the gas station, Alex gathered her into his arms and held her. Wordless, gentle, and with an air of patient understanding that reassured her this was normal, this was grief, this was having to live without the one person you always thought you'd have. This was pain and anguish. This was sadness because of all the firsts Martin would never see. All the firsts stripped away from her future, dropped to the bloody earth in a faraway land.

She cried, as she did on every anniversary, unable to speak or breathe, choking on the mass of impotent wishes that swelled inside her chest.

This year, unlike the ones that had come before, she wasn't alone.

24

Four

Monk

Alex waited for her tears to slow, for the sobs to become less heartbreaking. It took a long time, but eventually she stopped shaking, and her breathing evened out. He'd adjusted his hold on her a couple of times while weariness overtook her, Amanda's body slumping against him as her muscles weakened.

He didn't try to tell her it would be better, or that she'd get over it. He took the waves of grief that emanated from her body and absorbed them as best he could, giving her a safe place to pour out her pain.

Instead of telling her it would pass, he shared how his family had dealt with a loss like, and yet unlike, hers.

"When I was twenty-five, my younger sister went missing. I was deployed overseas in the sandbox, about to head home on leave, and got a text from my mom asking if I'd heard from Tracey. She was twenty-one and finishing up college, and my folks tried not to treat her like anything other than the grownup she was. They didn't keep tabs on her; it wasn't like that. But Tracey's roommate had called. She hadn't come back to the dorm, and a quick check with her professors found her absent that day. I looked back at my messages from her and found the last three had been a week earlier. Funny pictures and jokes that I hadn't responded to." Amanda made a sound and went to pick up her head, but he cradled her skull close with a quiet, "Shhhh," until she settled against his chest again.

"My folks got the runaround from the cops. Some song and dance about her being an adult, and sometimes people just got tired of their lives and left. She wasn't in a relationship, didn't have kids or a pet, didn't own a car or a house. A prime candidate to just pick up and vacate, at least in their eyes. Me and my folks, we knew different." He stroked Amanda's hair and knew by her stillness she was listening intently. It was good to take her out of what she'd been stuck in for so long, and even if it hurt to tell this, that'd be worth the effort.

"She was the good kid." He snorted. "Not like me, as I'm sure you can imagine."

Amanda did interrupt him then, and he smiled at the determination in her voice. "You seem plenty nice to me."

"Nice, sure. But good? Not always." He stared at the flagpole yards away, at the center of the graveyard. "Not hardly ever." With a quick breath, he pushed past those memories and continued on. "Tracey was the kind of kid who texted, even away at college. She kept the 'rents in the know with her life. Voluntarily, probably because they didn't demand it of her. Those texts, random things about food and friends, announcements that she was going out to parties, or made it home safe—they stopped the night she went missing."

"Oh no." Amanda pulled away, and he could feel the weight of her stare on him, even as he refused to meet it.

"Oh yeah." He cleared his throat, suddenly thick with tears. "Two weeks went past, and nothing. I got home finally, just in time. I was over at their place, helping organize the stuff volunteers needed, about to head out and put up posters when I looked through the window to see my folks' pastor pull up at the curb, followed by a cruiser. It was like I was frozen in the spot. I saw the men get out, watched the three of them cluster at the end of the sidewalk. I didn't get to the door before my mom, but I was there to catch her as she fell. Tracey's body had been found in a copse of woods close to the school's campus. Their best guess, she'd been dead before she'd even been reported missing."

"Oh, Alex. I'm so sorry." She patted his chest gently and he nodded, the movements rough and jerky.

"I don't know what was hardest on my folks. Knowing she'd been dead for so long, or the fact they didn't know she was already gone. Mom kept saying things like a good mother should have known." He shook his head. "Took the whole family a long time to come to grips with the fact sometimes bad things happen to good people."

"I'm so sorry," she repeated, and he ducked his chin to stare into her eyes. Red and swollen, they were welling with tears again. "So, so sorry."

"Sounds trite, I know." He shook his head. "Trust me, I know how it sounds, because I've bitchslapped myself for saying it to my folks, to mothers and fathers of men and women who served with me, but it's true. We can't control the bad things that happen, but we can work to get to a place where that acceptance doesn't tear us apart." He stroked the fall of her hair, smoothing out the tangles from when she'd been pulling and yanking at it. "You aren't there yet, but you gotta do the work and get there. You can't keep doing this to yourself."

She moved back, and his lap felt emptier than he expected. There was a biting chill all along his front, even in the heat of the evening. "I can't. I miss him so much."

He pushed up from the ground and dusted off his ass, then looked at the gravestone with the single name, no room for a spouse, and he wondered if she understood what that had meant when she'd purchased it. "You will, because you deserve to."

The rumble of his bike's engine and pipes was loud in the cemetery, and he sat for a moment fiddling with his glasses and bandana, settling everything comfortably into place. Numbing routine helped when the memories threatened to overwhelm.

Alex took a deep breath and turned to look at Amanda, still seated on the blanket beside her husband's grave, loss and confusion on her features. He offered her a brief two-fingered wave and idled out to the road. A different car than the one she'd driven yesterday sat in the parking lot, listing to one side on a low tire.

He pulled out onto the road and rolled the throttle, easing into the first gear change before laying into it and rocketing through the rest. He told himself that even with the glasses, it was the speed and wind that teased tears from his eyes, and he blinked hard.

Five

Amanda

She braked to a stop and looked around at the empty lot as she parked the car. Her gaze flicked towards the crest of the hill, searching, and she didn't know if she should be relieved or disappointed when no one waited for her there, either.

Blanket, water, and scrapbook in hand, she closed the door and shoved the keys into her pocket. Same car, different story this year. She'd gotten an anonymous gift certificate in the mail about six months ago for the local repair shop, and it had been more than enough to cover the work needed. No more half-done fixes; everything was running smoothly now. She just wished she knew who to thank.

At Martin's grave, she'd already spread her blanket and gotten set up before she noticed the addition. A crisp, new American flag had been placed next to the headstone, and the granite looked wet. She touched it with her fingers and lifted them to her nose, sniffing delicately. The liquid held the distinctive odor of whiskey.

Amanda looked around again, hopeful, even knowing she was alone. Tears slid down her cheeks. For today, this one day, she'd allow herself to feel the grief that never seemed to truly leave.

"I miss you."

She did, probably always would. But as the biker had promised, the past few months had crept around a corner somehow, and life had gotten easier.

"I got a new job. Did I tell you?" An opening had been posted on social media for a night manager at a local hotel. She'd stared for a long time at the pile of bills that never seemed to get any smaller and had called the next day to begin the application process. "Started last month."

She wiped both cheeks before picking up the scrapbook, and she flipped towards the back. As her fingers worked through the pages, she quietly told him, "That's why I haven't been here as much." The night shift hours were wrecking her head, but after nearly six weeks into it, she felt like she was finally in the groove. The first time she'd slept through her normal visit to the graveyard, however, she'd lost it, climbing into the shower in her pajamas and huddling under the spray, crying until the water ran cold. *I can't tell him that.* The illogical nature of her thoughts didn't matter, because on this anniversary of his death, for this span of time, these hours spent here one day a year, it was all his.

"Another local boy died a few months ago during his deployment. We went to school with his older brother." She flipped the pages until she found the one with the clipping. "There was a big honor ride, just like with you." Gently, reverently, she smoothed out the edges of the newsprint. "Alex was there. I didn't see him myself, but he's in this picture." She touched the image, careful to keep away from his face. She had two spare papers stashed in a crate at home in case she needed to replace the article inserted into the scrapbook, but she wanted to keep it as pristine as possible. "You remember him. He was here with me for a while last year."

After he'd left, riding away into the sunset, she'd curled up on the blanket and wept more, sobbing herself to sleep, awakened by the calls of coyotes in nearby fields. Cold and stiff, she'd gathered up everything and trekked back to the car. Alone.

She glanced at the flag. "Was he here before me?" He hadn't wanted to intrude, she remembered him saying that.

She remembered everything he'd said.

For the first month after meeting him, her dreams had seemed evenly split between Martin and him.

Martin's were always the same, movie reels of the milestones in their lives. High school prom, graduation, wedding, officer school graduation, first deployment. Known events, ones that made her smile upon waking, until she remembered and the reality of her life came crashing back in on her.

The ones featuring Alex had been different, more like an old Technicolor movie where the hero was a swashbuckling larger-than-life character, always setting out to save the damsel in distress. She was consistently cast as the damsel, and as weeks went on, her swooning reactions to his appearance became more and more erotic. She'd woken just yesterday morning with her hand in her panties, shocked to find an unfamiliar slippery wetness there when she changed her underwear.

Cheeks flaming hot, she ignored those thoughts as she flipped more pages in the scrapbook. This was part of the ritual she'd missed last year, and Amanda was determined to stay on track today. She began the familiar recital of all the things that made up their lives. "Do you remember when…"

A couple of hours later she was back beside the car, blanket held high in the air as she folded it into manageable squares. She heard motorcycles in the distance, coming closer, and clutched the material to her in anticipation. Nerves she didn't know she still had zinged through her chest and belly, and she turned to catch the first glimpse of the riders.

There, at the very front of the line of bikes, was Alex. His head turned and he gave her a graceful wave with his free hand. The riders behind him looked at her, heads swiveling to match Alex's, and a few hands rose in a similar wave. She lifted her hand in response, holding her breath until they'd completely passed by, the roar and thunder of their pipes fading just as quickly as it had swelled.

Hands shaking, she finished folding the blanket and tucked it away, then climbed into the car. Amanda sat there a moment, fingers tight around the steering wheel.

He'd remembered.

Six

Monk

The cemetery disappeared into the distance, and Monk settled deeper into the seat of his bike. Even without the reminder on his calendar this morning, he'd known he would be detouring the planned ride to pass by the place where Amanda's husband lay.

The past year had started out as a shitstorm of epic proportions. Blade had wrecked out, and for a couple of days it hadn't looked like he'd make it at all. Then the docs weren't sure if he'd be the same if he woke up. He'd proven them wrong, and Monk had been there beside him every step of the way, his arms the first to help his brother stand, his voice the loudest one arguing with the man when Blade wanted to give up.

There'd been plenty of that, too. In quick succession, he'd attended funerals of three men he'd served with overseas. Gun, drugs, and a bridge abutment had been their exits of choice, and he'd stood at the foot of each grave, back straight, chin lifted, trying not to see the faces of the family they'd left behind.

Just yesterday, Blade had thanked him, his tersely spoken, "Don't know what I'd'a done without you, brother," music to Monk's ears.

A year ago today, his brothers had asked where he'd been, and Monk hadn't offered the real story, instead giving out winks and nods that let them draw their own conclusions, all of them wrong.

Not that he would have minded their versions. Not at all, and his body had reinforced the idea since his cock stood at half-mast whenever he thought about Amanda. Not even needing one of the little blue pills he hoarded like a miser. Amanda in his lap? Boom, stiffy. Amanda smiling at him as she said the ridiculous word "ixnay" and yeap, stiffy. Amanda touching him, palm to his chest as she offered heartfelt condolences over the death of a woman she'd never met? Wham, stiffy. That one he'd acted on, and found the orgasm easier to chase, the ending more satisfying than any he could remember.

The BFMC had a support club in her town, and he'd used those contacts to keep track of her. When his man reported in that her car hadn't moved in days, he'd gone down to check it himself. The engine had a cracked head, and the tranny was trashed, all a result of hard driving in the vehicle's past he attributed to her dead husband. A quick recommendation by his man had Monk conducting a transaction at a local mechanic shop.

He'd slipped the envelope with the gift certificate into her mailbox himself, heart racing as he rang the doorbell like a kid doing ding-dong-ditch and sidled around the corner of the building. He'd held his breath as the door opened and closed, then opened again, and he'd heard the rattle of the mailbox.

He hadn't stayed after that. Made his way back to his bike and headed out of town, mission accomplished.

In the distance, he saw the diner he'd targeted for their meal stop and held up a closed fist in warning. A quick glance down gave him a glimpse of the still-white fabric of his new officer patch, and Monk's chin lifted as a swell of pride rose in him. *Wonder what Amanda would think*, he thought, as he turned on his indicator and patted the air in a "slow down" motion. When he'd met her at the gas station, she'd been terrified of him and his brothers. From what she'd shared graveside, her life had been tame and staid in comparison to his, and he smiled as he angled onto the blacktop of the diner's parking lot. She'd gotten over her fear—of him, at least.

Rumbling exhausts surrounded him, and he blinked away the shadows of nonexistent mountains, forcing his shoulders upright. Their road captain shouldn't be afraid, and he wouldn't let his brothers down. He parked and got off the bike, stretching as he watched the lot fill with all the bikes he'd led on today's ride. Blade and Neptune stood nearby, and he saw Wolf walking their way, an easy smile on his lips. *All my brothers.*

"Monk, hey Monk." He looked over to Blade and lifted his chin in response. "Was that the widow back there?" His chest burned and he opened his mouth to retort then closed it tight, unsure what this flare of anger and jealousy meant. *She's supposed to be just mine, not for him.* He shook his head and saw confusion on Blade's face. "No? You sure? It looked like her, man." His hands passed through the air, tracing an hourglass shape that had Monk gritting his teeth. "She seemed to know you."

He stared a moment, then dipped his chin and looked away. "Yeah, that's Martin Stewart's widow." Maybe if he didn't say her name, he could get through whatever his brothers would be throwing at him over the next few minutes without decking one of them. His mouth had other ideas, because it kept talking. "Today marks six years for him. I figured Amanda would be at the cemetery." *Jesus.*

"Amanda?" Neptune drawled her name slowly. "That's the widow?"

Monk pushed through their little group and angled towards the front door of the diner. "I'm gonna get a table before it fills up." They had enough men on the ride today that some would have to eat in shifts or get their food to go and have their meal outside. He glanced up at the sun, still high in the sky. It was hotter today than last year, and he wondered if she'd remembered to drink any water. She'd been leaving the graveside earlier than last year, and he thought that was good. *Jesus*. Here he was in the middle of a ride with his brothers, and Amanda still consumed every thought. "See you inside."

"Monk, hey Monk." He glanced over his shoulder at Blade, who was standing there with his hands out to his sides, looking more confused than before. "I piss you off or something, brother?"

With a sigh, he turned back and shook his head. "No, man. It's all good. Just hungry, you know?" At Blade's reluctant nod, he returned it and then made his way inside, ordering a drink and a burger.

Neptune was the first to join him, sliding onto the seat facing him with a low grunt. "Blade didn't mean anything by it."

"I know. It's no big deal." Phone in hand, he saw he'd missed a text from his mother, thumbing a quick reply as the other two men claimed their seats. "I got a burger," he muttered quietly as he flipped over to his social media. He did his best to maintain a low profile because of the club but used it to keep track of his family doings.

As he scrolled through his oldest brother's pictures of a recent picnic with the family, a friend request popped up, the bright, white number one flashing at him briefly. Blade and Wolf were debating the wisdom of a couple of prospects apparently ordering Mexican before getting back on the bikes for the last hundred miles planned for today, and he idly snorted a laugh at Wolf's graphic description of the mistake he saw happening right in front of him. At the phrase "exploding pants," he tuned the pair out and tapped the request.

Amanda Reynolds Stewart.

Reynolds must be her maiden name.

Clicking on her profile, he found few things were public. An old picture of her with a dog, an image of her husband's headstone, and an American flag posted last Veterans Day, thanking the troops for their service. He shifted uneasily when he read her relationship status still said married. Uncertain if he should accept, he was staring at her picture when the request went away, a message flashing across that it had been withdrawn.

She'd looked him up, and requested it, then backed out. Scared, maybe? If he hadn't been looking at the app, he might not have ever known it happened. *She wasn't afraid of me when I saw her last.* There was no reason for her to have changed her mind. *Dammit.* He punched the friend request button and watched the pending status for a moment, then locked the phone. *It's up to her, now.*

Seven

Amanda

An instant after hitting the button, she'd had second thoughts and retracted her request.

Now, she stared at the status on the screen with a frown drawing her brows together. It had changed again, so fast she nearly hadn't seen it happen. She'd just fallen to her doubts and canceled the friend request when it popped back up, but this one said decline instead of cancel, which meant Alex had noticed what she'd done and issued another request from his end.

She still had his profile page on the screen, and the pictures he'd been tagged in went on and on. Rows upon rows of family and friends who'd laid claim to him as theirs.

Either a brother or son, an uncle in a couple of cases, or a good friend—most of those had motorcycles in the background.

His relationship status said married. There was no name, and nothing in the images spoke to a significant other, but the status definitely said married.

He hadn't spoken about a spouse, someone special in his life, but to be fair, the single day a year ago that he'd spent with her had been entirely focused on her and what she'd needed to get through the hours spent at the graveside. He'd talked about the tragedy of his younger sister and how it impacted his folks. He'd shared a few memories of his time in the service, but nothing more personal than that.

Of course he's married.

A man that handsome, sensitive, and self-confident?

Of course he'd be taken.

She left the friend request where it was and closed the laptop, setting it aside.

Eight

Monk

Ass propped on a stool at the corner of the bar, Monk pulled out his phone. He was waiting on his brothers Blade, Neptune, and Wolf. Checking the time, he saw he was nearly half an hour early for their plans, which meant he'd be sitting by himself for a while.

"Hey, Monk. Want your usual?" He nodded, and it struck him then that he *had* a usual. He'd been here often enough to be recognized and known, his preferences marked and noted by the staff. He grinned when a line from an old sitcom theme song ran through his head. "Here you go." The full glass thumped onto the bar in front of him.

Monk grinned wider and lifted it, tipping the rim towards the bartender. "Cheers."

"Cheers, Monk." The man grabbed a bar rag and walked away, swiping at rings of condensation left where patrons had missed the coasters.

Transaction completed, he brought the glass of beer to his mouth and sipped, savoring the bite and chill after a long day working. Then he settled deeper into the seat and thumbed over to the social media app. Amanda's profile looked the same, but he found himself trolling her info, just in case. *Nothing new*, he thought, clicking into her friends list, cruising past portraits and avatars, images of kids, dogs, houses, cars, pausing on the rare motorcycle.

Nothing that would help him connect with her any more than he had.

This kernel of want had lodged in his chest. Lodged, found a place to take root, and was growing.

Something he didn't know what to do with.

So Monk did what he'd sworn to himself he wouldn't do anymore. He navigated to her limited pictures, pausing for long minutes over each, taking in Amanda's expressions, those smiles that didn't reach her eyes. He drained the beer, giving the bartender a nod for another. It didn't help the burn, that ember of pain deep in his gut.

He tried to ignore it, trusting his subconscious to keep picking at the problem until the solution would appear.

He'd only known about her for a year; she shouldn't be so important. *One year, eight months, thirteen days.* He shook his head.

Fingers flicked at the screen as he navigated to the private group the club maintained and responded to questions from members, then back to his public profile to engage with family, and back to his timeline to see what else was going on. Under a wash of notifications for his account was one he nearly missed. There, buried between various tags by his brothers and memes shared by his family, was a single line that said Amanda Reynolds Stewart had liked and commented on an image he'd posted yesterday.

Monk clicked on the picture, a closeup of him taken by Neptune's flavor of the day. He hadn't known she was taking pictures, so he hadn't ducked away from the camera, wasn't looking directly at it, either. His focus was farther out, somewhere out of frame, probably on something Blade was saying.

There were dozens of comments, mostly ragging on him in the way brothers did, or statements of fondness by family. Added in the mix was a single line of text by Amanda, saying simply, "Thank you for your service."

He liked her comment.

A moment later he came back and studied it again, finally touching the application to select a different response, one more fitting. He stared at the screen, the steady glow of the heart seeming to mock him.

Still, he left it.

Nine

Monk

The club was doing well. They'd grown in numbers, and Neptune had finally talked Monk into sponsoring a prospect, his first. The process had taken up more of Monk's time than he'd expected but felt good. He liked the role of mentor, passing on his wisdom to a baby biker, just as he'd done for the newbies in the service. He'd changed apartments, going smaller, just a single efficiency this time, because all he did there was shit, shower, and sleep. The rest of his days were either spent at work or with the club.

Monk took his duties as road captain seriously, wrenching side by side with members to get their bikes ready for a run. He'd personally knifed more tires in the first half of the year than he'd expected, because so many of the members just didn't pay attention to the condition of their own bikes. Wolf had gotten him a deal with a local racer, and the club had a stock of take-offs in the shed out back now. Tires too slick to race on but with plenty of tread to last at least a season for most of the men in the club.

So work and the club were both doing well, and if his personal life wasn't anything to write home about, he wasn't going to cry because his nights were spent alone.

Two days before the anniversary, he opened the social media app, prepared to stalk Amanda's profile as normal. He'd already planned what he wouldn't do this year and had quietly arranged to be working on the day. Nothing good would come of feeding his obsession with this woman, not when she was still tied so tightly to a dead man.

When he navigated to her page, instead of the three pictures, he found dozens. A wealth of images of her. Old and new, they tracked back to high school, and he smiled to see her as a teen standing awkwardly on a stage stuck inside a period costume that looked a mile too big. Her wedding picture was there, and the sight of it caught at his chest, leaving him aching inside to see her standing in white next to a man he assumed was Martin, her face shining with happiness.

Documentation of the kind of graduation ceremony he well remembered was there, Amanda tucked in beside Martin, the man standing ramrod stiff in his dress uniform, a shiny single bar on the epaulets of his jacket. *Butterbar.*

Monk smirked. He'd always hated that name. Another picture of just the man at some station overseas, his posture as casual as it ever got when surrounded by enemies, the mixed tans of the desert stretching for miles behind him, those damn dark mountains on the horizon.

He blinked them away.

She'd accepted.

After a year, she'd finally accepted his friend request.

He clicked through to read her posts, not overly surprised to find them sparse on real information. More a surface glossiness to keep family and friends at bay. A way to keep loved ones from asking too many questions, to satisfy their curiosity and dampen any inklings of concern. He recognized the tactic, because it was what he did, too.

Day manager is way better. Winky face emoji. She'd tagged a local hotel and he grunted in shocked recognition. He'd stayed there a few years ago when his bike broke down in a nearby town. It had been the only American-owned place within a reasonable distance. At the time, he hadn't been living in the area very long and didn't feel comfortable asking his brothers for assistance. Suck it up and make do had been his motto back then.

He frowned, following the thought of him then to his responsibilities in the present day. If his prospect had done the same, Monk would be pissed as hell, because it would show a lack of faith in his brothers. *Dammit*. He'd need to do a better job of modeling the behavior he wanted to see. *Lesson learned.*

This movie is the best. Red heart emoji, thumbs-up emoji. There was an image accompanying that post, a selfie of her with a movie poster in the background. Monk sucked in a surprised breath and smiled. He'd been to see that movie on opening night, suffering through the shouts of "nerd" from his brothers as he drummed up company to go with him. She was alone, still smiling, but he thought he could see tiny cracks in the façade. They were there in the way her smile didn't reach her eyes. In the forced quality of that smile. Compare it to that damned wedding photo, and it was clear that she was still hurting.

In the profile summary, he saw something that had him stumbling mentally, trying to find a foothold on his emotions. Then he was dialing his manager, asking for a favor and getting it. A last-minute schedule shuffle to give him an unexpected day off.

Relationship: Single.

Ten

Amanda

Heart in her throat, Amanda carefully steered her car into the parking lot she'd become so familiar with over the past seven years. It was empty, as was usually the case, and she tried not to let disappointment overwhelm her. She knew once the tears started, they wouldn't stop until she was wrung dry, no matter what set her off.

She killed the engine with a twist of the key, then sat with her head resting on the steering wheel for a moment. Just another anniversary, and no reason for her to believe it would be any different. On the one hand, she was kicking herself for waiting so long to accept his friend request, and on the other hand, she knew it didn't matter that he'd remembered the day for the past two years. Martin hadn't been a friend or served in the corps with Alex, so there was no reason for him to come here.

Leaning over the seat, she gathered up her supplies. A new, thicker blanket this year, after a boisterous puppy she'd fostered had chewed holes in the previous one. A water bottle instead of a bottle of water, and she smiled slightly at the distinction she made in her own mind. Renewable was the new trend, and it made sense to her, so she'd stopped buying cases of water, instead depending on the filter she'd attached to her brand-new kitchen faucet.

That was another change, bigger than most of the rest of them. She'd saved her money, and between the better pay at the hotel and help from an unexpected insurance payout, she'd signed papers and put a down payment on a little house at the edge of town. Nothing big or showy, just two bedrooms. Still, it was hers in a way she'd never had before. Following their wedding, she'd moved straight from her childhood bedroom in her parents' home into a garage apartment at Martin's folks', then into the house he'd wanted. She'd never had a space that felt like it was just hers, and she liked it. If she wanted to paint the kitchen, she could, and there was no one to tell her no.

Of course, there was also no one to help, but she'd shoved that knowledge into a compartment deep in the back of her mind, ignoring the ping of hurt every time she muddled through something alone.

Same scrapbook, with new pages in it to document her life. There was one with a newspaper ad for the job that had started her on the current path at the hotel. And another with a picture the real estate agent had taken of Amanda holding the keys to her new house, broad grin stretching her mouth.

Amanda had talked about the scrapbook with another widow at a survivors group she'd started attending and thought the words given her had been profound. "Maybe it's a way to remind yourself that keeping on, continuing to live, isn't bad. Maybe it's a way to find things to celebrate in your life now." She'd reached out to touch Amanda's arm, and for a moment, it was as if the woman's tiny tattoo had glowed as bright as a supernova. Amanda had stared then turned her own arm over, showing the matching symbol etched into her skin. They'd clung together and wept, and exchanged numbers, the first time Amanda had done so since Martin died.

Set apart from the rest of the pages were the things she'd done to document Alex's life, too. And that was something she'd intentionally decided to not think about, why she felt the need to keep tabs on him and his friends.

Two whole pages were taken up by the six front-page photos of his club escorting bullied kids to school. Another two pages had been dedicated to the club itself, everything she could find out about it. History, original members, their occasional brushes with the law balanced against the many donations from them to animal shelters and veterans' memorials. Even the colorfully painted benches now scattered along the local nursing home sidewalks were a gift from his club.

She'd drawn the line at including anything specific to Alex, but that hadn't stopped her from stalking his social media, scouring every picture for a glimpse of his elusive significant other, that status of Married never changing.

With a deep breath, she pushed open the car door and stepped out, arms filled with the items for her vigil. Head down, she trudged up the rise to where Martin's grave was, each step harder than the one before. She'd never felt like this before, as if coming to see him on the anniversary of his death was a chore, something to get through. It was never pleasant, but she'd always believed it her duty. He was gone, and she was here, so she mourned him the only way she knew how. With tears and grief, and devotion.

She'd never know what caused her to look up.

One moment she was lost inside her own head, wallowing in grief for the death of someone she'd loved, and for the loss of so much of herself, and the next she was staring at Alex as he finished pouring something on the dirt beside Martin's headstone. He lifted the flask and took a long drink, staring at the nearby flagpole where the American flag proudly flew. His bike sat where it had the first time he'd come here, and she stood where she'd been the first time she'd seen him here, and he was about where he'd been then, too. It was like a surreal overlay of the then and now, and she was dizzy with the idea that maybe she'd imagined these past two years.

Then he turned and faced her, and she saw the differences he bore. His beard was thicker, darker and filled out along the jawline. There were lines on his face that hadn't been there before, and when he smiled at her, she knew where they'd come from, because the creases exactly matched the expression of pleasure he immediately showed her. His smile was real, and honest, and something she hadn't known she needed until she saw it.

Alex had filled out in other ways, his shoulders even broader than before, and she wouldn't have been surprised if he'd had to get a new jacket just to fit all of him. She adjusted the blanket, too conscious of the fact she'd filled out, too, and not in ways she liked to think about. After Martin had died, she'd lost all the remnants of baby fat she'd carried through school. She hadn't thought about the fact that the process had reversed until she'd recently had to retire her favorite pair of jeans when they'd gotten too tight everywhere.

"Hey," he called, voice low and rasping, as if he'd been here awhile without speaking.

She nodded, not sure her mouth would work right now. *Why is this so awkward?*

He gestured towards the grass where they'd sat last time. "Here okay?" Another nod was her only response, and he looked at her intently, head cocked to one side.

"Amanda, if you'd rather be alone, I can go. I…" He trailed off, and then laughed softly. "Honestly, I'm not real sure why I'm here."

"Please, stay." He smiled at her again, and her breath caught in her throat. "I'm glad you're here." She dipped her gaze to his boots, then back up to his face in time to see a satisfied smirk cross his face. "You look good, Alex."

"You do, too." He made a show of inspecting her as he reached for the blanket. They juggled things for a moment. Then he had the material spread smoothly on the grass. "I'm glad you accepted my request."

Amanda paused in midcrouch, one hand and knee on the blanket, and looked up at him. "I'm sorry I took so long." *Is he flirting with me?*

"All good things take time." He made himself comfortable on one corner, feet stretched out to the side, arm locked behind him as he leaned back. He held out the flask. "Want a drink?"

She shook her head. "It was you, last year, too, wasn't it?" He didn't respond, just looked at her. "It was still wet when I got here. I couldn't have missed you by much." She gestured towards the dark spot on the dirt where he'd dampened it with the whiskey from the flask. "What does that mean?"

"Libations for the fallen." He lifted the closed flask. "Drinks for those who can no longer imbibe, those gone ahead to Valhalla. It's an old tradition and for some reason felt right when I was here. We might not have served together, but together we served, if that makes any sense." His shoulders made a small movement, a stretching roll that exposed discomfort. "A brothers-in-arms thing, I guess."

Amanda hurried to reassure him he hadn't overstepped, hadn't offended. "I think it's touching, and very fitting." She reached out and laid her hand over his for a moment. "Thank you."

They sat in silence for a few minutes, the sun growing more intense overhead and baking through her thin shirt. She could only imagine how hot he had to be in the jacket, but he didn't move, didn't give any indication of discomfort.

"It's weird, you know?" She didn't look at him. "There's a grasshopper, right there on your toe, and it didn't exist last year when I was here. That bird"—she gestured towards a starling hopping along two rows over— "probably didn't either. Not last year, much less the last time Martin was breathing and home." She sighed. "I lost the house he bought. Did I tell you that?" He made a sound and she nodded in embarrassed admission. "He loved it a lot, had all these plans in his head. It was okay, not my dream home, but it sure was his. He would have been so mad at me."

"Why would he have been pissed?" She glanced at him to see his head back, closed eyes aimed towards the sky. "Gonna be blunt here, Amanda. He's the one dead, not you.

You had to make decisions that were right for you. Keeping a house that you didn't want in the first place would have been stupid." His head rolled to the side, and he cracked open one eye, his gaze cutting. "You don't strike me as a stupid woman."

She stared at him as he resumed his sunbathing. "Aren't you hot?"

"Yeah, but I ain't got no shirt on under the jacket. Figured it was the least of bad choices to just keep it on." The same head roll, same cracked eye, and he was staring at her again. "If it won't bother you, then I'll lose the jacket for now."

"It won't bother me." She laughed softly. "I appreciate your consideration, but I'd rather know you were comfortable."

"Alrighty then." He sat up and shrugged, the worn leather falling easily down his arms, and she stared, and stared, drinking in the sight of him. He was covered in tattoos. Front, back, arms, neck, everything she could see had ink either on or adjacent. The one on the side of his neck she'd seen before, a glimpse that first day at the gas station, a moment so far in the past it seemed surreal that it had brought them here. He had a winged eagle that spanned his shoulders, talons reaching far down his spine, the head wrapping cunningly around one scapula. His arms were a mixed canvas of tiny tattoos and larger pieces, all intertwined with vines and words and colors that probably meant something to him but looked like beautiful chaos to her. One pec held a replica of the emblem from the back of the jacket, and she noted how it was reverently separate from other tattoos. Set apart somehow by being isolated, and she liked that he gave it a place of honor. His abs flexed, and she tried to read the words arching over his bellybutton in between his stuttering breaths, finally giving up as she realized he was laughing. "Woman, you get your fill of lookin' yet?"

She stared at his face because his smile was blindingly bright, eyes twinkling at her as he gently poked fun at her scrutiny of his body.

"Oh, God. I'm sorry." She turned to face the headstone as he got to his feet, then cast a glance over her shoulder at a sound, afraid it was him leaving, but he'd just draped the jacket across the seat. Folded so the symbol for his club was hidden from view, he took a moment to ensure it was stable and wouldn't fall on the ground. "Is it like the flag?" He glanced back at her with a question in his eyes. "The jacket. It's your club insignia, right? Are you not supposed to put it on the ground?"

He smiled, but it was somehow cautious, as if she were treading along the edges of something that wasn't her business. "Yeah, something like that. What do you know about a motorcycle club?"

She shook her head with a laugh. "Just what I've watched on TV."

"So, not much," he teased with a grin as he sat back down, closer to her than before by inches. She watched the muscles in his arms and back play under the skin, mesmerized at the movement underneath the colorful pictures. After a few moments, he asked, "You ever ridden?"

"What?" She blinked and shook her head. "Uh, no. No."

"Lemme know if you wanna change that status." For a moment, she fixated on the social media status she'd impulsively changed a couple of days ago, just prior to accepting his friendship. He narrowed his eyes and clarified. "From nonrider to rider."

Of course he didn't mean relationship, you idiot. He's married.

She whipped her head back to the side and stared at Martin's name etched in stone. It was engraved in the wedding band she no longer wore, too.

That had been the first change, about a year and a half ago. She'd gotten out of the shower and picked it up to slip onto her finger, where it had ridden since Martin had placed it there standing in front of his friends and family. She'd hesitated, then set it back down in the little tray she kept in the bathroom for that purpose. After it remained there a month, she'd moved it to her nightstand, and after weeks there, to her jewelry box, tucked back into the foam and velvet alongside her impractical engagement ring.

She'd done it without much thought, just accepting it as a change and moving on. Now she wondered if it meant more. If it had been her first unconscious decision to begin moving forwards and out of the stasis she'd been caught in since his death.

"Amanda?" Alex's question was cautious, careful. "Did I say something wrong?" She shook her head. "Are you sure?" That one she simply didn't answer, keeping her blurry gaze on the stone, no longer able to pick out Martin's name. "Oh, honey." If she hadn't been weeping before, the sweet pain in Alex's voice would have caused it. "Come here." Then he gathered her up in his arms, like he'd done before, and arranged her in his lap. This time it wasn't leather under her cheek, but warm muscles covered by silken skin. She closed her eyes to block it out. Block everything out. "I'm so sorry for your loss."

She couldn't have answered him if she'd tried, throat closed tight with tears and regret. If she could have, she would have told him it wasn't Martin's death that caused her to weep but the impossibility of building anything with Alex himself. *So stupid.*

"Lost one of my soldiers to an IED. Years ago. There wasn't enough to put in a box to send home to his folks. Hands down, that was the hardest call I had to make, first notification I had to do. I got home in time to go to his funeral, a memorial service, and they had pictures of him everywhere. Helped me to see what he was, before." The sound of his heart steadied her, a regular bump, bump, bump in her ear. "Caught up to his girlfriend a couple of months ago. She's married now, two kids, a good life, you know?" The thudding sped up slightly. "She looked at me for a single moment and I could see it all crashing back down on her. My fault for being in the grocery store. My fault for being someone who'd known him. Her face went white, and I swear she was just a minute from passin' out." The thudding was faster yet, and then his hand settled on her back. She sighed and nestled closer, and his heartbeat evened back out, slowing to the same steady thump, thump from before. "I told her how good it felt to see her honoring him by living her life. Not sure she believed me right away, but I said it again, and again. How it isn't right to lock up the sweetness that's still here and hold tight to that bitterness of loss. I think that's something you need to hear, too." He adjusted his hold on her, the underside of his forearm banding across the side of her breast, and just that innocent touch was enough to make her stomach swoop and dip. "It's okay to live, Amanda. It's okay to want things that you didn't have together. It's not going to change anything if you stay stuck. Well, it will. It'll change you, but not for the better. So if you want to try new things like ridin' on a bike, you just let me know and I'll tell you it's okay, and normal, and makes me happy. That's you bein' strong, and that's a good thing to see."

"You're married." She winced at the words bursting from her traitor mouth, blurting things she had no intention of saying.

"What? No. No I'm not." His arms tightened around her, wrapped tight as he could without crushing her. "Not for years now." She didn't argue, let him have this denial, and felt the change in his body when he realized what she meant. "Oh, fuck. Honey, no. She divorced me long before

I left the military. Hated being left alone, and what she got of me wasn't enough for what she needed. Then I got out and, hell, I'm so different. There ain't no way I'd put up with her shit now. Plus, she's married again. I just never changed it because…fuck, I don't know. It would make a statement, you know? Put a pin in it, and everyone would know. I mean, they already know, but I just didn't…" He shifted under her, and she went with the jostling, letting him roll to one hip and then back.

From the corner of her eye, she watched him shuffle his phone hand to hand, then wrap the empty one around her again as he worked on the device with the other. "There," he said with finality, bringing the screen closer. She blinked. Status: Single.

"Alex." She started to say something, not sure what, but certain her traitor mouth would come up with what she needed.

He shook his head. "Nuh uh. You hush, now. That's not for you, that's for me. Swear." A repeat of the movement as he put the phone away. Then he had both arms around her again. "For me."

His heart beat steadily underneath her cheek, reassuring her that this hadn't been traumatizing, that he wasn't conflicted, that it didn't matter to him, except how it mattered to her.

Eleven

Monk

The sun was edging towards the west, and still, they sat. The skin on his shoulders had tightened with a burn he knew he'd feel later, but damn, the way she'd looked at him would be worth any number of inconveniences like a little sunburn. She'd eaten him up with her eyes, and thank God she'd been stuck on all his bared skin, because he'd popped much more than a stiffy, every part of him puffing up under her regard.

The sense of relief at figuring out what was bothering Amanda still swirled through him, part exhilaration and part fear, because he didn't want to fuck this up. At some point over the past two years, this woman who should be virtually a stranger had become critically important to him. Today may have marked only the third time they'd spoken, but each of the conversations had been so weighty, so filled with important topics, that it was as if he'd known her forever. Like he knew her inside and out, and she him.

It had been a long time coming, but today felt like a beginning, and he wanted to hold on to that as long as he could.

Twelve

Monk

It had been a rough day at work, but Monk enjoyed how his crew pulled together to overcome obstacles. Made him feel good about being bumped up to supervisor, and he was pleased to be assigned such good men. Beer in hand, he checked his messages and smiled to see one from Amanda. After months of occasional exchanges via social media, which had gradually grown more frequent, and then edged into flirting territory, she'd asked for his phone number. ***It's just easier***, she'd messaged, following it with a tongue-sticking-out emoji.

And he'd acquiesced. Sent her the number only a fraction of a second after her explanation message, desperately fast if she'd noticed.

He scrolled up to reread the first message in their string. It was from her, of course, because he stupidly hadn't asked for hers, just handed his out like candy. And then she hadn't messaged right away. Which meant the resulting interval of two days had been killer on his nerves. He'd been too stubborn to go back to the messaging app and prompt her, stuck in a merciless kind of limbo where it felt like his future hung in the balance.

Then she'd texted, and he'd spent long minutes trying to read subtle messages between her questions, because she'd gone straight for deep and personal. He'd balked for a moment, self-preservation instincts prompting him to hold back. Then he reconsidered, remembered the welcome weight of her in his lap, took a deep, deep breath and answered in full, giving her everything she wanted to know.

Why did your wife divorce you? Just the time apart doesn't seem like enough of a reason, so saying it that way feels like a cop-out to me. Was she unfaithful? Were you? I know this probably is something like date fifteen territory, but it doesn't feel like I've ever not known you, and I want to know. I want to know before I take any steps with you. Do you still love her? Is that why you didn't change your status for years? Years, Alex. That's not something you put off by a week or two. My counselor says not making a decision is making a decision by default, even if it's a decision to deny whatever it is you're avoiding. And by you, I mean me. Anyway, this is long, super long, like a book already, but I wanted to know. If you want to tell me, that is. Oh yeah, this is Amanda, in case you haven't figured it out by now. Serious face emoji, slight smile emoji, question mark emoji.

He'd started with the easiest response.

I knew it was you right away.

She didn't text back, and he didn't blame her, because he hadn't addressed the questions she'd already said were important to her.

She sent me an email to announce I'd be getting papers. I tried to call her, but it went to voice mail. I wasn't unfaithful. I didn't cheat. I'd never do that to someone I loved. If I love someone, I'm all in. No backing out from me. Do not pass Go. Do not collect anyfuckingthing.

He'd paused a moment, but there was no answering bubble to indicate she was typing, so he'd forged ahead.

The corps was a good fit for me. Semper fidelis *fit my personality. Fits. Always faithful. Friends, family, my brothers in the club. Did I tell you that you get points for always calling it a club and not a gang? That shit pisses me off.* He'd been getting off track and had scrolled back up to reread her questions to make sure he answered all of them. Even the ones she didn't know she was asking. *When I got out of the corps, it wasn't my decision either. That was hard, too, like the thing that defined me didn't want me anymore. My wife didn't want me, my career didn't want me. I didn't even get on that damn website for a few years. By then she'd unfriended me, changed all her settings and deleted all the photos of us together. It felt like one more slap in the face, you know?*

He'd hit Send and sat, staring at the screen in his hand. It had seemed like forever before that little bubble appeared. It was only when he'd blown out stale air from his lungs that he'd realized he'd been holding his breath, waiting. The bubble went away, then came back, that cycle happening twice more before her message appeared.

Oh, Alex. That's terrible. She didn't even wait to do it face-to-face, but EMAILED you? He could have almost heard her outrage in that capitalized word and had smiled. *If anything at all was wrong while Martin was deployed, I held it close until he got home. I didn't want to break his concentration, you know?* He wondered if she knew she was echoing his typing style with the question at the end of a statement. *Semper fi is more than words, it's a way to live. That's how I understand it, so the fact you were faithful doesn't surprise me. It pleases me to no end, but doesn't surprise.* A warm sensation swirled through his chest at the idea that he'd pleased her. *I'm so, so sorry that I made you answer all these things, Alex. It's so unfair of me, and you would have been within your rights to tell me to go jump in a lake. Thank you for not telling me to go jump in a lake.*

He'd just begun typing a response when another message came in. Alex had sat and stared at it for a moment, then, with a broad grin on his face, had replied differently.

PS – I'd like to change my status someday soon. Winky face emoji.

This was a request he'd known he would bend over backwards to make happen for her.

How about tomorrow?

God, that first ride had about done his head in. It had been one thing to intellectually know she'd be perched on the seat behind him and another thing entirely to experience it. Heat from her legs alongside his hips had branded her presence into him like a welcome mark. Her enjoyment of the experience had been exhilarating, and he'd known instantly he'd never be the same. The trust she exhibited was addictive, and through the months since then, he'd initiated rides even when he didn't really have the time, stealing away from club functions to be with Amanda.

No regrets. He tapped at the screen with his thumbs, issuing an invitation that he knew she wouldn't turn down. *It's time.* Pulling in a deep breath, he flipped over to another chat string and reached out to his brothers, giving in to their often stated request to officially meet this woman who had so consumed him.

Blade was the first to respond, and his ***Hell yeah*** made Monk grin. Wolf followed quickly with an ***I'm in*** that Monk acknowledged with a thumbs-up emoji. Neptune's answer was slower coming, but when it did, it held all the support and love he'd come to expect from the BFMC members. **Monk, brother, you want us there, we're there**.

So fuckin' lucky.

A message came in from Amanda, so he navigated back to their thread, grinning at her proclamation: **It's a date**.

It was past time to take things further with her, with them, and he couldn't wait to show her how he truly felt. Didn't matter how the idea of it made his stomach clench; he needed more with her. He'd loved her for months now, even without a single kiss shared between them. Monk had learned her breathtaking beauty paled in comparison to the strength she carried inside, and every interaction between them only made him want her more.

For months he'd steeled himself every time he dropped her off at home, because he longed to touch her, hold her, kiss her, love her.

Only days from now, he'd finally act on it.

Thirteen

Amanda

She waited at the curb, hands clasped in front of her chest as she watched Alex ride towards her. He never wore a helmet, but as usual, she saw the one she thought of as hers strapped to the seat behind him and smiled fondly at his thoughtfulness.

He rolled to a smooth stop right in front of her and shook his head. She could hear him chuckling at her excited reaction over the rumble of the bike. His low call of "You ready, honey?" stirred heat in her belly, and she pressed a clenched fist tight to hold it in.

They'd ridden together at least once a week since she'd messaged him her request. The first time was terrifying and thrilling all at once. She knew now that Alex had taken it super easy on her that first ride, because since then, they'd ridden on more challenging roads and even on the interstate. She'd been afraid to look at the speedometer that day, staying huddled close against his back. As she'd gained confidence, he'd ratcheted up the length of the rides, too. Today would be another first, because they were supposed to join a group of his friends for part of the day.

When he'd dropped her off two days ago, she'd asked him in as she always did, and he'd demurred, but with a different response than his standard and frustrating excuse of, "Gotta get home, honey. Work tomorrow." Two days ago, instead of the normal, he'd told her, "You still want me to come inside Saturday, I'm down for that." From the look on his face, he'd meant more than those few words, which was how her hopeful heart had taken it.

And now it was Saturday and she'd almost rather they not ride at all, skipping straight to the part where he came inside. But he already had the helmet loose, was handing it to her while he did something on his phone. She realized he hadn't killed the bike. All a clear signal that he was in a hurry for some reason, and she didn't want to disappoint him.

Helmet in place, she put her hand on his shoulder as she stepped onto her pegs. Hers, because this seat behind him was hers, too. He'd told her at the start of summer that she was the only woman who'd ever ridden behind him, and in her mind, she wrote forwards in time to try and impose her wishes that she be the only one. *Ever.*

She wrapped her arms around his waist and snugged up to his back before calling out, "Ready."

What had started out as the most innocent of touches, a need imposed on her by safety's sake, had turned into an intimacy she longed for. Hours spent with her thighs pressed tight to his hips, arms around him, and Alex giving her the protection of his body. This was what had led to her wanting him to come inside, wanting more, but he'd dragged his heels, capturing her fingers with his hand the one time she reached for his face. The only kiss that had passed between them happened that day, the beard-rough feel of his mouth against her knuckles as he'd shaken his head. His muttered promise of "Soon" hadn't warmed her bed, but she'd held to the fact it wasn't a no.

He patted her leg and they were off, the bike jerking in a familiar way under them as he worked up through the gears, topping out a handful of miles per hour over the limit. She'd never felt unsafe with him and knew the speed kept them moving with traffic, something she'd never considered important before. But a slow bike was a vulnerable bike, subject to being overtaken by a distracted driver.

Time passed along with the scenery, flashing by in a smear of greens and browns. More touchy-feely than normal, she noticed Alex kept rubbing and stroking her hands where they crossed his belly, fingers threading through and gripping, squeezing and then rubbing and stroking again. Almost as if he were trying to soothe her. *Or himself.*

He slowed, and she sat up to look around. They were pulling into a gas station where three bikes were already parked in front of the store. Butterflies struck hard then, and she felt unsure of herself for a moment before shaking it off. *If he didn't want me to meet them, he wouldn't have invited me today.* The men stood and started strolling towards them as Alex parked. "You want me off the bike?" He nodded, but she wasn't certain if it was in response to her question or in greeting to the men. Then he touched her leg, a soft stroke, before holding his hand out. Answer enough, so she used that leverage to clamber off the bike.

"Brothers, this is Amanda." Alex stepped off the bike and stood next to her, his posture stiff and uncomfortable. "Amanda, these are my brothers. Blade, Wolf, and Neptune."

She nodded and smiled, aware of the measuring gazes on her. Then the man called Blade grinned broadly, and she huffed out a surprised laugh because he looked delighted at something. "Damn, Monk, this girl's too pretty for you."

Alex hadn't relaxed, still ramrod straight, so she bucked up her courage like she'd done the first time she'd texted him and wiggled in against him, not stopping until his arm was over her shoulder. She threaded her fingers through his, like he'd done earlier, and gave him a squeeze. "Oh, he's the pretty one. I've got the catch of the year here."

Acceptance and appreciation flashed over the faces of the three men, followed by laughter. "Gas up, brother," said the one called Wolf. "Then get your pretty lady back on the bike and let's ride."

79

Fourteen

Monk

Couldn't have asked for a better day. He glided them to a halt at the curb, then changed his mind and swung back out into the street. Amanda's fingers clutched at his shirt at the unexpected movement as he turned to ride up the drive and onto the flat pad just in front of her garage door. *Might as well make a statement she can't misunderstand.* He'd already promised her things would change today, and with the way she'd responded, confidence and uncertainty in the same breath, he wanted to see where this could go. *No more dropping her off at the curb. No more watching her waving form grow smaller in the mirror. No more hearing her huffed sigh of disappointment as I say goodbye.*

She stood up off the bike and looked at him, and just that attention had his dick perking up. Because, if the smile on Amanda's face was any measure, she not only hadn't mistaken his intent, she was entirely on board with the idea. Then she parted her sweet lips and asked him, "Come inside?"

Alex took her in for a moment, fingers clasped in front of her belly, twisted into a complicated knot he wanted to solve. Her bottom lip disappeared, then slowly released as she raked the flesh with her teeth. *She's nervous*. Probably just as nervous as he'd been to introduce her to his brothers, his friends, his corps here at home. Not that he'd expected they'd do anything to embarrass him, but it had mattered that she liked them. She'd met that challenge head on, making it clear to everyone how she felt about him, and her willing actions had gone a long way towards settling his gut. She fit, and his brothers knew it as well as he did.

Now it was his turn to set her at ease. Alex got off the bike and stepped closer, shuffling forward until their toes met and she had to stretch her neck to look up at him. Lips parted, she stared into his eyes, waiting. *Gonna stay out here for this first one*. What he wanted to do wasn't something he was ashamed of, nothing he wanted to hide. *So fuckin' pretty*. Fingers to her chin, he cupped her jaw in his palm and ghosted a caress over the apple of her cheek with his thumb, the difference between her satin skin and his calluses stark. *So fuckin' sweet*. Then he leaned in and pressed his lips to hers.

Amanda sighed under his touch, mouth moving under him, and she opened sweetly when he touched the tip of his tongue to her lips in gentle exploration. Minutes passed as he kissed her, as she kissed him back, as the stars turned and wheeled overhead, and something in the world clicked into place for one brief moment.

She was panting when he pulled back, and he was the same, breaths coming hard and fast. Alex smiled as she reached for the door.

He let her lead him inside, then closed the door firmly, shutting out the world, closing her in here with him.

"Alex." His name was a breath on her lips as she turned, fingers still twined with his. Two strides separated them, and he covered the distance quickly, swaying to a stop in front of her. It felt like his insides were quaking, and with fingers shaking, he lifted his hand to her face, framing her smile.

"Amanda." The curl of her mouth broadened, spread, and he felt the heat from her open mouth on his lips when he leaned in close. "I got a want inside me." She was the one to cover the distance this time, traveling that final inch to press her lips to his.

"We'll save the house tour for later, then."

Eyes closed, he fell into her kiss, exploring every inch of her mouth, dueling with her tongue in a sensual slide and twist. *Bam, stiffy,* he thought, and smiled. That happened with her. He'd ridden hundreds of the best and most uncomfortable miles with her wrapped around him on the bike, his cock beating time on his zipper to come out and play. Lifting their joined hands, he brought her fingers to the notch of his throat and gave a squeeze, sighing into her mouth when she abandoned her hold to wrap around the back of his neck. He trailed the backs of his knuckles in a light touch down her other shoulder, past her elbow to find her fingers spread, waiting on him. He gripped and squeezed, huffing a laugh when she returned it with a pleased hum far back in her throat. "You wanna touch me?"

"Oh, yes." Her whispered response was immediate, gratifying in its eagerness, but threaded through with a tinge of shyness that told him he had to take care with her, always. *As if I'd do anything but.*

Pressing her palm against his chest, he covered her hand with his. "Here?" Her fingers spasmed under his and slid down an inch at his urging. "Here?" The grip on his neck tightened and relaxed, nails scratching lightly at the base of his skull. At his urging, her other hand slipped down another few inches, nearly to his waist. "Here?"

"Alex." He thought he could get used to hearing his name like she said it now, softly and filled with more plea than complaint.

Fingers wrapped in the back of her shirt, he pulled her towards him as she arched instinctively, their hips meeting in the middle. Heat seeped into him everywhere they touched, and Amanda's lips parted when he pressed his stiff cock against her, breath speeding its way to a pant. "I got a want for you, Amanda. I want you." He knew this house was hers alone. Martin had never been here. His ghost wouldn't be waiting in any corner to trip her up. But Alex also knew she hadn't been with anyone since Martin died, which meant her dead husband would be in her head. He wanted to exorcise him before they got to the naked part of the evening so it would be just him and Amanda in her bed. "You want to stop at any time, for any reason, I'm not going to be pissed. I treasure what we've got, what we're building, and it's worth the wait. I just wanted you to know that, honey. You're worth the wait, if you want to put the brakes on." He flattened his palm against her lower back, grinding against her lightly. "I've played this out in my head a thousand ways, and not one of them disappoints, so no matter how this goes down, I'm where I want to be. I'm not willing to lose you, any part of you. I like what I've got—and, Amanda, I need you, so don't think you'll run me off if you tell me not yet."

"Silly man." She tipped her head back and found his eyes with her unflinching gaze. "You've been the one holding back. I've wanted you for a long time, Alex Waterman. You'll not get out of bedding me that easily."

From her smile, she'd expected his snorted laugh. "Bedding you? That's how you're describing what I wanna do?"

"I want too, Alex. But the one way sounds too crude for what I want to do with you." She hesitated, and he saw uncertainty in her expression before she shrugged lightly and finished, "The other way to describe it, I'm not ready for." A pause, so tiny it could have been missed, but he didn't. "Yet."

"Yet." He echoed her word softly and she nodded. "But maybe?" Eyelashes brushing the rising red of her cheeks, she nodded. "Someday soon?" Her chin angled towards her shoulder, neck arching as she nodded a third time. "Where's the bedroom, Amanda?" He gripped her hand and stepped back, pleased when she swayed forwards against the loss of his body. A short hallway led off the living room, and he angled that way. Two doors bracketed the end of the hall, and at her direction, he opened the one on the left, towards the back of the house. Then they were in the room, door closed, shades darkening the weak rays of the setting sun, and he turned to her, lowering his mouth to hers.

Alex allowed his possessiveness and passion to roll through him, transferring to her with every touch as he stripped her bare. She stood before him, pale skin glowing in the low light, and he made quick work of undressing, kissing her between movements and gathering her to him when they were both naked.

She groaned as his arms tightened around her, lifting, then sighed against his mouth when he swept the covers out of the way and positioned her on the bed. Desperate for the touch of her bare skin, heat blazing along every inch of him, Alex stretched out to cover her, his hips falling between her open legs as he buried his face against her neck. "God, this. Just *this*, Amanda."

"Alex." Her palms grazed his sides, one traveling up, one traveling down, until her fingers curled around their destinations. She pulled as her hips lifted and he ground down against her, rigid cock trapped between them. Her nails scratching along his scalp, he went along when she urged his head to turn, and their lips met, mouths open and tongues tangling. They kissed until breathless, until he was rutting against her, ridge of his cockhead pressing and rubbing against her pussy, her clit, wet and heat and Amanda all around him as he slipped and slid against her.

He paused with a groan and muttered, "Condom." Utterance as much a wake-up call for himself as a question for her, he didn't expect any response.

"I'm on birth control."

Alex lifted his head and looked down at her, hair spread across the pillows, pupils blown wide and dark with passion. "You are?" That shy angle of her chin towards the point of her shoulder made him understand, but he needed to know. "For this?" She licked her lips, puffy and reddened from his kisses. His, no one else's. *Mine.* "Amanda, when did you go on BC?"

She raked her bottom lip between her teeth, cheeks again flagging red when she confessed, "Four months ago."

Two months after they started riding together.

One month before she'd asked him in the first time.

Certain of the answer, he still asked the question. "For me?" She nodded, and he angled his hips to drag his cock up between her pussy lips again, grazing across her clit. "You want this?" She stared at him for a long moment, then lifted and pressed her mouth to his, fitting against him as if they'd always been together, as if there'd never been anyone before him. *As if there'll be no one after me.* Determination filled him to make that thought into truth.

He stroked up, then down, down, down until the head of his cock caught at her entrance. "I want no one but you, Amanda." On that proclamation, he pushed in, her tight heat wrapping around him, pulsing against his shaft as she quaked inside. In, then out, then in again deeper, repeat, repeat, until an eternity later he was buried inside her. "You didn't want to put a name to it earlier, but I'm gonna tell you right now." He rocked deeper, her hips rising up against him, drawing him down. "This is me making love to the woman I want to spend the rest of my life with." She made a helpless sound, wound her arms around his neck, and pulled. Alex went easily, wanting nothing more than to kiss her senseless as he loved on her.

They kissed as he moved over her, as she lifted and fell beneath him, as they came together in an act that felt natural and right, and something he wanted to do again and again. Faster then, chasing her orgasm first, he pushed up on his arms to look at her. He told her to touch herself, wanting to see that, to feel how she tensed at the first tentative brush of her finger against her clit, the heat from her hand between them, and captured her fingers in his mouth on a demanding suck afterwards. The tight clasp around his dick never lessened, the slick glide into her wet heat never flagging.

Alex dipped his head and pulled her nipple into his mouth, sucking hard and finding her so responsive there he brought her to a second peak just before he lost control. Pounding into her, the knowledge she'd be sore later had his inner caveman roaring with pleasure at the idea that she'd feel him afterwards. Then something tipped inside, and heat that had been coiled and waiting at the base of his spine rocketed through his chest and limbs. Dancing sparks filled the edges of his vision and he kissed her through it all, groaning his pleasure down her throat. Her arms and legs wrapped tight around him while he plunged and thrust erratically, finally going deep and holding as his cock pulsed and throbbed.

"God, Alex." The strained murmur was the first thing he heard over the pounding of his heart. "I love you, too."

Elbows braced on either side of her head, he stared down at her beautiful face. Strands of hair stuck to one cheek, she was covered in sweat just like him and looked sated and happy. "You do?"

She pressed a clenched fist against her stomach. "I feel it here." Palm spread over her chest, she said, "And here." Her hand lifted to his face, fingers trailing through his beard before cupping his cheek. The graze of her thumb swept across his lips. "I love you."

"I'm so fuckin' glad. Nothing I wanted more." Leaning down, he dragged his lips along the edge of her jaw, pausing when his mouth was next to her ear. "You make me fuckin' happy, Amanda. So happy."

Fifteen

Amanda

She shifted restlessly as she woke, sheets a silken glide against her legs. There was a huff of air against the back of her neck, and she smiled when a large hand landed on her hip, sliding along her skin until it cupped her breast. Heat all along her back was testimony to a level of cuddling she hadn't expected from Alex. His breathing settled again, slowing as he drifted deeper into slumber. A glance at the clock on the nightstand revealed they'd only been asleep an hour or so, and she wondered what had woken her.

After not sharing her bed with anyone for years, she supposed it could just be the novelty of having another body in her space. She shifted again and sighed contentedly when she recognized the gentle throb between her legs.

Alex had expressed a pleased surprise after round two, pulling her close and gifting her with more of his history. She hadn't known about the ED issues, and the idea of him dealing with that alongside his PTSD was troubling. He was a good man, the best, and deserved so much more.

Alex jerked, making a low, pained sound far back in his throat, and his hand slipped away as he rolled to his back. "No." The guttural refusal filled the room. "Fuckin' no, brother."

She turned to face Alex, keeping her distance. Martin had nightmares sometimes, and she'd painfully learned not to startle him awake.

"Hold on." Garbled and roughened with emotion, Alex's voice sounded tortured. "I told you to hold on." His hands worked into and out of fists, almost as if he were trying to keep a grip on something. "Fuckin' hold, man. Hold."

As she had with Martin, Amanda tried to insert herself into the reality playing out in Alex's head. "Alex. You're safe. I promise, you're safe. You're with me. You're here, home, with me." His head jerked to the side, closed eyes aimed her direction, and his labored muttering paused for a moment. "I promise, you're safe, Alex."

His body seized, every muscle visibly tightening. Then the tension rushed out of him with a whoosh of air and he blinked at her before shoving to a sitting position. Wrist propped on his knee, he wiped at his face with his other hand. "I hurt you?"

"What?" Amanda was disconcerted at his rapid awakening and immediate lucidity. Martin had always fumbled around in that half-sleep state for minutes before fully waking.

"Did. I. Hurt. You?" Alex angled his face towards the door, away from her.

"No, Alex." Amanda shook her head. "You were talking was all. I just tried to help you wake. You didn't hurt me, not at all."

"You sure?" His voice was uneven, ragged and filled with pain. "I didn't hurt you?"

"No. No. You didn't. Promise."

"What the fuck are you doin' all the way over there, then?" His head swiveled and Alex stared at her, eyes reddened from the emotions he was still suppressing.

Amanda moved to him then, straddling his hips with her knees and wrapping both arms around his shoulders. Alex folded himself around her, face buried in the crook of her neck, and a moment later, she felt the wet there.

"I'm here, Alex." Cheek pressed to the side of his head, she held him tightly. "I'm here."

It took a while, more than an hour by the clock, but he eventually was soothed by her touch, her mouth, her words. The shaking in his limbs slowly faded until all that remained was exhaustion. At some point they'd shifted around in the bed, lying on their sides, pressed close together. It was in that position, skin to skin, that he gave her his secrets. The men he'd saved, forever altered by the cost of war. The men he'd lost, faces turning pale and gray under his gaze.

Their voices trailed to nothing, his stories coming to an end followed by a final repeat of Amanda's reassurance that she was there, with him, always with him.

"Pretty heavy stuff for our first time." Alex sighed deeply, the air in his lungs blowing out in a long stream over Amanda's shoulder.

"Pretty heavy," she agreed and tightened her hold when he would have moved away. "You've been carrying this for a long time."

Silence greeted her statement before his hair brushed against her neck as he nodded.

She smiled with love for her strong, silent man. And then marveled at the thought that he was hers. *He's mine.* "I've got you, Alex. Thank you for trusting me to help. Let me carry it for a while."

His great strength broke her grip, and he shoved back far enough that she could see his face in the dim light. Alex stared down at her for a moment, his gaze darting from one eye to the other, then dancing across her features before coming to rest on her lips.

"I've got you," she promised, and Alex dipped closer. "I've got you." This was softer, in deference to the proximity of his mouth to hers. "I've got you." The final sounds were lost when he captured her lips in a deep, demanding kiss that seemed to ask everything of her.

She offered the answer he seemed to be looking for, a quiet murmur against his mouth before he rolled on top of her again.

"I'll always have you."

Epilogue

Amanda

"Baby, you ready?" Alex's voice was slightly gruff as he leaned into the car, one hand on the roof.

She smiled at her reflection in the mirror over the visor, then adjusted it slightly to the side. Bright green eyes stared back at her from the back seat.

"Yeah. I'll be right out."

It had been three years since the ride that changed both their lives. Two years since they'd stood in front of friends at the courthouse and listened to the driest recital of vows ever conducted, something they still laughed at, making fun of the fussy man with the bowtie. And it had been only three months since she'd watched Alex openly weep as he cradled their newborn daughter in his arms, his expression full of wonder and love.

She'd asked him last night if he would rather she go to the cemetery by herself this year, then laughed when he sounded affronted she'd even make the offer.

"What? Oh, hell no. No, baby. Me and Marty are comin' with." He looked up from his position on the floor next to their cooing baby.

"I just know it's not the most pleasant of days." She shrugged.

"It's an important day." He winked at her, then turned back to Marty and booped her gently on the nose, laughing softly when she squealed. *"We'll be there with you. Gotta see what you've added to the book."* His voice rose an octave. *"Don't we, pumpkin? Gotta see what Mommy's done this time."*

She stepped out of the SUV and turned to face Alex, smiling and shaking her head when she caught him sniffing the baby he'd retrieved from the back seat. He claimed new baby smell was addictive, and if his behavior was any indication, the man was well on his way to being hooked.

Amanda opened the rear door to gather the blanket and scrapbook, which was now overflowing with added pages to document their lives. Alex was right; she was always adding to the book. Her sleeve shifted, and she caught sight of the revised tattoo on her wrist. A year and a half ago, after they'd decided to try for a baby, he'd held her hand as she went back to the tattoo artist who'd done the original. Now, the semicolon made up one edge of a continuous line drawn in the shape of a heart. To her it represented the fact that life—and love—would always go on. She gathered everything and stepped back to close the door, staring across the roof at her husband, her daughter, her family—found and made with so much work and pain and love, and she couldn't imagine not being here in this moment, right now.

"Alex?" He looked up, one eyebrow quirked at her. "Thank you for your service."

A shadow flitted across his face, and the muscles of his arms tensed as he held Marty closer. He still had dark days, but he told her they were fewer and fewer, said she was his salvation, redemption at the end of a long, hard fight.

"I love you, Amanda Waterman."

Part of her heart would always belong to Martin. Their lives had been too long entwined for it to be otherwise, and she wouldn't give up a moment of the time she'd had with him. Alex, though, had helped her begin a new chapter, in more than one way. She cradled the scrapbook to her chest.

After Martin had died, part of her had gone to sleep— the piece that always demanded more, that wanted to grow and belong—and love had lain dormant for years. Alex had woken her up.

Amanda and Alex were carving their own path, far different from anything she could have dreamed. Her own personal hot, tattooed biker wouldn't have it any other way. He challenged her every day to look for the good. And when he needed her to, she pushed him, too. Good days or bad, they were all made better just by being together. She looked at him again to find his face still buried in the crook of their daughter's neck. *My bad boy.*

~~~

~~~

THANK YOU SO MUCH FOR READING
Service and Sacrifice!

This story is book #1 in the Borderline Freaks MC series, and is best enjoyed as a prelude to book #2, *More Than Enough*. Featuring Blade, that story is one you're going to want to read to get to know this man better, trust me. He's a good'un.

ABOUT THE AUTHOR

Raised in the south, *Wall Street Journal* & *USA TODAY* bestselling author MariaLisa learned about the magic of books at an early age. Every summer, she would spend hours in the local library, devouring books of every genre. Self-described as a book-a-holic, she says "I've always loved to read, but then I discovered writing, and found I adored that, too. For reading...if nothing else is available, I've been known to read the back of the cereal box."

Want sneak peeks into what she's working on, or to chat with other readers about her books? Join the Facebook group! **bit.ly/deMora-FB-group**

deMora's got a spam-free newsletter list she'd love to have you join, too: **bit.ly/mldemora-newsletter**

~~~~~
~~~~~

Borderline Freaks MC series

This series is comprised of four stories, and are best read in order to avoid spoilery situations.

Service and Sacrifice

"Thank you for your service" is what we're taught to say to military men and women in gratitude for our freedoms won at their expense. Less often do we thank their families, those left behind to hold down the fort, to manage the day-to-day struggle of keeping everything up in the air until their loved one returns.

When you can't count on anyone else to save you, there's only one real choice.

Amanda lost her husband to war. Alex lost part of himself. Through a series of glancing encounters, Amanda and Alex find reasons to continue on. And together, they'll discover hope and peace can be found in the most unexpected of places.

books2read.com/serviceandsacrifice

~~~

More Than Enough

When a man sees himself as damaged, imperfect, and flawed, it's hard to believe there could be love in his future. After a near-fatal accident stripped Blade of his confidence, he didn't hold out much hope ... for anything.
~~~

Until Jenn—gorgeous, sweet, and kind—dropped into his life.

Where he sees destruction, she sees perfection.

Where he sees helplessness, she sees courage.

Where he sees ruin, she sees strength.

Can he ever believe he's more than enough?

books2read.com/morethanenough

~~~

Lack of In-between

Wolf finds Rose harbors more secrets than he expected, and the deeper he pulls her into his life, the more he likes it.

Once a man's been embedded in the bloody aftermath of battle after battle, with no relief in sight, he's forever changed.

Wolf came home from overseas to find his world askew. He was no longer a husband, since he and his ex agreed they were better friends than partners. But he still held the coveted position of father, an experience so confusing and rewarding it sometimes left him breathless.
~~~

He's got a lot on his plate personally, and even more with the Borderline Freaks and the challenges he and his club brothers have hit lately.

He just doesn't have time to make room for a relationship.

Right?

books2read.com/lackofinbetween

~~~

See You in Valhalla

This is Angelo Dobbs' worst nightmare. A good man lies dead, and with their president and founding member gone, the leadership position within the Borderline Freaks MC falls to him.

It's not that he can't manage the easy task of leading a group of good men; he would just have preferred to stay a little farther out of the spotlight. But, when his brothers issue the call, he answers.

Carly Gibson, daughter of his dead friend, is an unexpected—but not unwelcome—complication for his new role. She's the most intriguing woman he's ever met, capable and filled with a strength of character. He finds himself instinctively drawn to her. Could he have found the woman meant to complete him, finally?
~~~

Over the past couple of years, Dobbs, Neptune to the men of the BFMC, has watched as his closest friends found their soulmates. Now, their women are an integral part of the club, and when they and Carly are threatened, Neptune will do anything to ensure their safety—and just maybe, his future.

books2read.com/seeyouinvalhalla

Other Motorcycle Club Romance Series

My Rebel Wayfarers MC and the Neither This Nor That MC series do cross over, along with the Occupy Yourself band books, so readers have a couple of choices. The series can be read independently beginning with RWMC, OYBS, and then NTNT without too many spoilers. There's also a crossover between my RWMC world and Lila Rose's Hawks MC world. Or they can be read intertwined—in chronological order.

Here's the recommended reading order if you want to follow according to timing:

Mica, RWMC #1

A Sweet & Merry Christmas, RWMC #1.5

Slate, RWMC #2

Bear, RWMC #3

Born Into Trouble, OYBS #1

Jase, RWMC #4

Gunny, RWMC #5

Mason, RWMC #6

Hoss, RWMC #7

This Is the Route of Twisted Pain, NTNT #1

Gypsy's Lady, RWMC #11.5

Thunderstruck, NTNT #5

Going Down Easy

No Man's Land

Cassie, RWMC #12

~~~~~
~~~~~

Also by MariaLisa deMora

Neither This Nor That MC romance series

Legends are born from moments like these. Folktales spun around a single point in time so perfect, you can almost hear the click resonating through the universe as things align. Meet Twisted, Po'Boy, Retro, and Ragman, good old boys from southern states who have many things in common. First, is a bone-deep love of the biker lifestyle. Second, would be their love of the brotherhood, and knowing that you trust the man at your back. Finally, these men have the love of a good woman. None of these come without a price, and it is our pleasure to journey along with them as they discover the blessings that can be won, and lost along the way.

This is the Route of Twisted Pain
Treading the Traitor's Path: Out Bad
Shelter My Heart
Trapped by Fate on Reckless Roads
Thunderstruck

5-Star Reviews for the stories of the NTNT MC series

This is the Route of Twisted Pain

"This is the Route of Twisted Pain is an exhilarating, gripping romance novel contrived of incredible world building, complex yet relatable characters, and a unique, captivating plot.

Gifted storyteller MariaLisa deMora beautifully balances exciting suspense, fast action, intriguing secrets with delicious, blazing hot romance scenes.

Readers will be up all night with this riveting page-turner."

~ NY Literary Magazine

I am completely tickled in my fancy for TWISTED!

First off, let me state that there was one thing I didn't like about this book and that is the LAST PAGE! I hated for it to end. I dearly loved this book and its characters as well as their setting.

~Colleen M.

Gripping tale

Twisted and Penny fit together beautifully. The book covers so much more than just their love story. Great introduction to the Incoherent MC. The tale is gripping and gritty. The journey is full of twists and turns that keep you on the edge of your seat. I couldn't put it down. Cannot wait for the next one.

~Lillmil

Twisted is one of the most original and interesting characters I have read in a long time. Marialisa's character building is setting a high bar for her to follow, she will hopefully continue with Po'Boy's story. The Route of Twisted Pain was pure brilliance, and I highly recommend this read.
~Penny T.

This book obsessed me!
This may be the best book I read all year.
These people...they're not characters, they're real... have stuck in my head from the day I met them.
MariaLisa deMora can throw words down that'll Twist (hehe) your insides up till you can't breathe for waiting to hear what's next!
I'm working my way through her other 'families' and yup...she really is that good.
~DeLane

Treading the Traitor's Path: Out Bad

"Treading the Traitor's Path: Out Bad is a solidly engrossing, well-written novel by a talented author.
MariaLisa deMora delivers a thrilling ride filled with exciting suspense, deliciously explicit, vivid sex scenes, and gritty, fast-paced action. Her characters are smart, complex, and strong with sharp edges. The settings meticulously detailed.
Fans of Motorcycle Club romance stories will not want to miss this second installment in deMora's exciting series."
~ NY Literary Magazine

Book Hangover
What an amazing read! DeMora does not simply wrote a book, she pulls you into a different world. When you read her work, you are very much surrounded by the characters and setting. Prepare for a book hangover because once you finish the book, you will still be stuck with Po Boy.
~KW

More More More
THIS WAS AMAZING. Highly recommend for a good story line, interesting characters. I just wish there was more more more.
~Laura

Loved This Book!
What did I just read?! Is my kindle still working? I'm pretty sure it combusted into flames while reading this story. RED HOT READ for 2017. Not what I was expecting at all! I tend to stay away from ménage a trois, because for me it's hard to say there's any kind of conflict except for jealousy, and the ending kind of leaves things unresolved and unrealistic. NOT THIS BOOK! The best one out there guaranteed.
~Linda A

So Freaking Good
...seriously this series is just WTF so freaking good. Dark, Twisted, harsh, painful and raw. Po'Boy lives for his club, his brothers and his family, there is nothing he wouldn't do for them.
~Fay

The author delivers a 5-STAR READ
I live and breathe for books like this! Fabulously Naughty!...Wickedly Hot! This is my first book by MariaLisa deMora and it will not be my last. MariaLisa delivered a 5 STAR READ! The plot is filled with action, suspense, romance and tons of hot scenes.
~Jenny F
~~~~~
~~~~~

***Alace Sweets*, a dark romantic suspense standalone**

A dark thriller, this book is not a light read. Filled with edge-of-your-seat suspense, this intense story commands the reader's attention as it drives towards the explosive ending. Alace Sweets is a vigilante serial killer, with everything that implies and is sure to trip all your triggers. Be ready.

At seventeen, Alace Sweets turned a corner in her life, taking the wrong shortcut home from school.

Resisting the harsh knowledge her attackers will never be made to pay for their actions, Alace takes a stand. Justice must be served, and if fate's scales are out of balance, she's determined to set things right as best she can.

When the laws of men fail, the rules of Alace prevail.

5-Star Reviews for Alace Sweets

"Whatever deep dark trench [deMora] pulled a character like Alace from should be revisited again and often."
~Confessions of a Serial Reader

"deMora has a superb story-line and exceptional character development. All of her characters have such depth that will intrigue the reader..."
~Turning Another Page

"Hot, sweet, dark thriller."
~Beth D

"It will keep you on the edge of your seat and give you chills."
~Escape Reality Book Blog

"Disturbing, haunting, sickly; yet hot, sexy and heart racing!"
~Amanda L

"From the first page [deMora] pulls you into the world she has created and you do not even try to escape..."
~Little Shop of Readers Blog

"A must read for all those dark, gritty romance fans out there."
~Sweet & Spicy Reads

"You will find yourself so drawn into the story that the outside world is blocked out and your locking the doors and turning on all the lights."
~Danena F

"Don't judge me for bonding with a vigilante serial killer, she's more than what she does."
~iScream Books

"Thrilling...chilling...full of suspense, nail biting edge of your seat excitement."
~Tracey H

"Every time MariaLisa deMora picks up her pen (or opens her computer), she creates characters you want to believe in."
~Gail S

"Intriguing dark storyline, beautiful love story and nail-biting conclusion, what more could a reader ask for?"
~Manda M

"This book takes you a dark and twisted ride that is gripping..."
~Renee Entress' Blog

"This book is dark and gritty and I literally had to take a day off from reading it because it's that intense."
~My Girlfriend's Couch

"This is my favourite book so far from this author ... I recommend this book if you enjoy dark romantic thrillers."
~Cheekypee Reads and Reviews

"There's not enough stars to give this book and 5 just doesn't really do it justice!"
~DeLane C

"I couldn't put this book down from page one! Tried to stop & go to bed but couldn't sleep thinking about Alace and got up & finished the book."
~Debbie M

"MariaLisa DeMora, wordsmith that she is, made this a story of the enlightenment of a woman and finding love in a life where she has had none."
~Kat W

~~~~~
~~~~~

Hard Focus, a criminal thriller standalone

This is an intense page-turner, a gut-punch twist-filled story about a woman who has confidence in herself, believes she's a good judge of character, and has filled her life with people she can trust. She's right, but she's also very, very wrong. Readers will have a time of it trying to decide who to watch closest.

Where do you place your trust when your own instincts betray you?

Connie Rowe is a receptionist at a respected legal firm. She's a little bit sassy, a lotta bit happy, has good friends, and is adored by her neighbors.

Life is good.

She's got a boyfriend she enjoys spending time with. He can be a little intense, but he's got a lot going on in his own life, sorting out his young daughter and nightmare of an ex.

Life is grand.

"Trust your gut." That's what Connie's police officer father told her often, training his daughter to believe in herself through the years.

But … what happens when you can't? When your intuition lies?

What happens when things come into Hard Focus?

5-Star Reviews for Hard Focus

"Hard Focus is one very well-written tale. 5 stars is not enough for me."
~Tabitha

"What a powerful story. [deMora] kept me invested from the first word to the last."
~Jesse R

"[deMora] has a certain magical touch to writing her characters, that they become either your nemesis, your best friend, or your love interest. That is certainly portrayed in this spin around. Loved it, loved it, loved it."
~Sandy K

"I strongly recommend this book for both entertainment and to broaden your knowledge of certain laws that must be revisited."
~Words Turn Me On

"An intense page turner. Once you start, you can't put the book down."
~Tracey H

"A beautifully written, powerful read that I can't rate highly enough. This story will stay with me always."
~Gayle

"This book had twists I didn't see coming. Loved it!"
~Lori R

“Wow! I am in awe of deMora's skill in crafting this story.”
~Kat W

“I keep sayin that there just aren't enough stars to give to some of Marialisa deMora's books...this one is no different!”
~DeLane

“Where do I start with this one...I read this in 3 1/2 hours uninterrupted, I absolutely could NOT put it down. Very deep, keeps you guessing, what's gonna happen next, kind of book. I love how strong her characters are, especially the females!”
~Wendy I

“Sometimes I feel like MariaLisa deMora is the one I should be watching out for. I started reading her books because I'm addicted to MC Romance, but then she decides to change things up and I just follow her wherever she leads me like a Pied Piper. I never know what to expect, and sometimes I'm afraid to find out, but it's always an adventure.”
~Rosa for iScream Books Blog

“A plot full of twists and turns, a story that's not quite what it seems, strong characterization, jaw dropping revelations... what more do you need from a book?”
~Manda M

ADDITIONAL SERIES AND BOOKS

Please note that books in a series frequently feature characters from additional books within that series. If series books are read out of order, readers will twig to spoilers for the other books, so going back to read the skipped titles won't have the same angsty reveals.

Rebel Wayfarers MC series:

Mica, #1
A Sweet & Merry Christmas, #1.5
Slate, #2
Bear, #3
Jase, #4
Gunny, #5
Mason, #6
Hoss, #7
Harddrive Holidays, #7.5
Duck, #8
Biker Chick Campout, #8.5
Watcher, #9
A Kiss to Keep You, #9.25
Gun Totin' Annie, #9.5
Secret Santa, #9.75
Bones, #10
Gunny's Pups, #10.25
Never Settle, #10.5
Not Even A Mouse, #10.75
Fury, #11
Christmas Doings, #11.25
Gypsy's Lady, #11.5
Cassie, #12
Road Runner's Ride, #12.5

Occupy Yourself band series:

Born Into Trouble, #1
Grace In Motion, #2 (TBD)
What They Say, #3 (TBD)

Neither This, Nor That MC series:

This Is the Route Of Twisted Pain, #1
Treading the Traitor's Path: Out Bad, #2
Shelter My Heart, #3
Trapped by Fate on Reckless Roads, #4
Thunderstruck, #5

**Rebel Wayfarers & Incoherent MC
(NTNT) crossover stories:**

Going Down Easy
No Man's Land

Mayhan Bucklers MC series:

Most Rikki-Tik, #1
Mad Minute, #2
Pucker Factor, #3
Boocoo Dinky Dau, #4 (TBD)

Borderline Freaks MC series:

Service and Sacrifice, #1
More Than Enough, #2
Lack of In-between, #3
See You in Valhalla, #4

**If You Could Change One Thing:
Tangled Fates Stories**

There Are Limits, #1
Rules Are Rules, #2
The Gray Zone, #3

Other Books:

With My Whole Heart
Bet On Us
Alace Sweets
Seeking Worthy Pursuits (TBD)
Hard Focus
Dirty Bitches MC: Season 3

More information available at **mldemora.com**.